Kate's whole world just turned upside down. She's hearing weird things, and seeing weird things. And Mama Lucy is a witch. No, really. Not like a capital B witch, but a capital W witch. And the guy Kate's just saved from imminent death is half-demon. And the guy that's after her is a dragon

Her life redefines teen drama.

Craig's a half=breed, bastard son of a demon king. And he's a thief. He's just found the item he's supposed to appropriate when his cousin stabs him with a poisoned dagger.

Forrest is out to collect the bounty for capturing the bastard son of a demon king. He doesn't plan to save the girl, or the half-breed demon. He also doesn't plan to be the one who needs saving.

This unlikely trio find themselves chased by enemies, known and unknown as they slip into a different dimension called Burnt World.

RIVALS

Dragon Reign

KIT BLADEGRAVE

DEDICATION

Thank you to the readers!

❦

Sign up for Kit's Newsletter to find out about new releases.
Put the following in your browser window:
mailerlite.com/webforms/landing/m5q3f7

❦

Covers by Ammonia Book Covers

1

KATE

From this high up, I could see the world laid out before me. The fields beyond the town, the barns, and farmhouses. I could see for miles in all directions, soaring higher to reach above the clouds.

The air was cooler up here, but I liked it, the rush of the chilliness against my skin and the feeling of being utterly alone.

And free. Free from the darkness of my past and the not knowing what was going to happen in my future.

The moon was my only companion as I circled around, wanting to stay forever within the clouds and not have to touch down again. In some part of my mind, I knew this was all a dream, but I never wanted to wake up from it. Not that my life was all that bad, but I certainly wasn't free to fly.

I was larger than life here, above the world, but all

dreams must come to an end. I faltered in mid-air and suddenly crashed down, spiraling out of control.

Down, down, down—

I shot upright in bed with my heart pounding in my chest as I gasped for air. I was in bed, safe and sound, not ready to die as I hit the ground from such a high height. With a groan, I flung myself back onto my pillow and glared at the dull ceiling above me.

I missed the moon and stars already. As I lay there, I rolled my shoulders trying to ease the weird tension built up in them. But it didn't go away and instead grew worse. I turned over, but when that didn't help, I rose thinking standing would make it stop.

It didn't, and I stood in front of the old dingy mirror on my dresser, rubbing my neck and wondering if I was coming down with the flu. My body ached in weird places, and my arms were exhausted as if I'd been using them all night.

"Kate! Are you up yet?" a voice called from out in the hall. Mama Lucy.

"Yeah, I'm up," I replied. "Be out in a minute!"

"Get your sisters up," she yelled back.

I grinned and hurried to get dressed. They weren't my biological sisters. No one in this huge old mansion was related by blood. We were all taken in by the woman we called Mama Lucy. I came here nearly ten years ago when she found me wandering the streets alone. That's how most kids wound up here. She took us in without a second thought, homeschooled us, fed and clothed us.

She was our Mama Lucy.

I was the oldest in the house now. Those who used to be my age, had moved away, ready to be on their own, but many sent letters and visited every now and then. As I'd grown older, I'd wondered how she managed to take care of us all. I never saw any social workers come to the house, or any checks in the mail from the government.

All the kids made up stories of where her money came from, that she had a treasure hoarded in the basement, or she was really royalty, but ran away and came to live here instead. The stories changed every year. Part of me cared to know, but another part didn't. She gave me a home, and I was grateful.

"Mary? Judy? Time to get up," I said as I opened the door to the room next to mine.

Two little girls, one blonde and one a redhead, sat up to stare at me with drowsy eyes. They were twelve and thirteen.

"It's too early," Mary grumbled and tucked her head back beneath the covers.

"No, it's not. Come on, you don't want to be late for breakfast, do you? The boys will eat all the bacon again," I warned.

Mary and Judy leapt out of bed at the mention of bacon, and I laughed as they darted past me, racing for the bathroom down the hall.

I loved mornings in this house, listening to the

hustle and bustle of the other kids and hearing Mama Lucy's laughter and talking.

"There she is," Mama Lucy said the moment I entered the dining room.

It had a long table that could fit twenty and was mostly filled already.

She kissed the top of my head in greeting. "You don't look like you slept well, dear."

"Eh, weird dreams," I said, finding one of the empty seats.

"You've been having a lot of weird dreams," she mused. "Anything on your mind?"

"No, not really," I lied. I always had things on my mind, like why I kept having these weird sensations that someone else was in my head, or why my dreams went from flying to utter nightmares.

"Hmm, I'll make you some tea tonight. Maybe it will help."

I thanked her and reached for the plate of waffles and grabbed a few pieces of bacon.

Mama Lucy hummed as she walked around the table, making sure everyone had enough to eat. Her vibrant purple shawl draped over her shoulders, and her black skirt billowed around her bare feet. She might look frail, but that woman was strong. She was stern with the kids she took care of, but she held her own against anyone who tried to give us crap or tried to buy out her home.

We were surrounded by businesses and modern-ized buildings on all sides, but her home remained.

Men in suits stopped by at least once a month trying to threaten her with legal actions to get her to sell the property or at least upgrade it, but she stared them down, and the other kids and I would watch from the windows as they bolted for the street.

But that wasn't the best thing about Mama Lucy. She was also a witch.

None of the younger kids knew that, and I was one of the few older ones who understood what she did, or at least what she believed in. Protective charms hung on all the windows, stars and bells, to ward off dark spirits. Several cabinets were off-limits to the kids, out in the greenhouse, but they were only filled with the herbs she grew, dried, and bottled, herself.

Most of what she did was for teas and soaps, lotions, and things like that. Natural items she sold at the farmer's markets, and through the tiny online shop she set up. Most of her orders came by mail, something I always teased her about.

She offered to show me how to make certain teas to relieve various symptoms a person might have, and even taught me words of protection—if I believed in that sort of thing, she would always tease at the end of our random lessons.

Whether she was a real witch or not didn't bother me. She was the only mom I'd known. The only parent I had since Dad died.

I lost my appetite thinking of him and pushed back from the table to take care of my morning chores in the greenhouse before lessons started for the day. All the kids had chores once they were old enough to help around the house. I liked being in the garden and the greenhouse the most, so Mama Lucy let me take care of her veggies and herbs.

"These are delicate plants," she'd told me. "They need love and care, not just water and to be weeded. These plants pick up on a person's emotions. You must always be aware of yourself when caring for such fragile things."

I took her words to heart, and before I entered the greenhouse, tried to leave behind any dark thoughts of the day I lost my dad. When I failed, I turned to the garden instead, hopeful that tugging some weeds out would help ease the pain blooming to life in my chest. I pulled on my work gloves from the fence, grabbed a spade, and went to work. I weeded around the tomato plants and the peppers, moving down the rows of vegetables, but apparently, this wasn't a good enough distraction. Soon I was lost in the memory of that day.

The worst day of my life...

"Katie! Get away from the window!"

"Daddy, what's going on?" I asked, standing on my toes to try and look outside.

He was there and shoved the curtain over the window. "You can't let them see you! Hurry now! Grab your bag and come with me."

I picked up my backpack and held his hand as he tugged me through the house. "Where are we going?" He was scared. I'd never seen him scared before and it terrified me. I heard shouts outside and car doors slamming. "Daddy?"

"Hush now," he whispered as we neared the back of the house. He crouched before me. "Do you remember what I told you?"

I stared fearfully towards the front of our tiny cottage that was meant to be safe out in the middle of the woods. My bottom lip trembled, and tears sprang to my eyes.

"Katie," he whispered sternly. "Do you remember?"

"The bracelet, never take it off," I recited, staring at the silver bangle with the gold runes set in it around my upper arm. "Never speak my last name to anyone. Never return to where we've stayed before."

He nodded.

The voices grew closer, and he pressed a finger to his lips, holding me close.

I held his gaze and jumped when they pounded on the front door but didn't scream.

"You go out to the woods," he whispered on a breath. "You go to your hiding spot, and you stay there until morning. Do you understand?"

"You're coming too, right?" I replied, but from the hard look on his face, I knew he wasn't. "Daddy."

"Do as I say and do not use your flashlight."

More pounding, followed by angry curses made him stand and shove me towards the back door.

"Now go! Quickly and do not come back, no matter what you hear!"

He shoved me out into the night and closed the door behind me as I heard the front one crash open.

I took off into the darkness, dashing into the trees behind our cottage. Yelling sounded from the house, but I didn't stop. I rushed through the trees, dodging them as they appeared out of the darkness. Tears streamed down my cheeks, fearful for Daddy, but I did as he said. I ran, and I ran until I found the rope ladder by the large oak. I climbed up quickly and hauled it up after me. I hunkered down in the hollow of branches. We couldn't build an actual treehouse, no matter how much I begged. Daddy said we had to be able to hide and anyone could find a treehouse.

I tucked my head against my knees and waited, but for what I didn't know.

Silence fell over the woods. It was late fall and cold, but no birds fluttered in the branches, and there wasn't even a whisper of wind. Just my ragged breathing as I peeked through the branches. I wondered if it was safe to go back even though Daddy said to wait until morning, but I thought of those men yelling. They were going to hurt him, I knew it.

Just when I found my feet, a bright white light exploded from where our cottage sat. A roar, it was like giant monsters, deafened me. I stared in awe at the light until it hurt my eyes and sank back into the safety of the tree branches. I waited there, shaking and terrified, unable to move.

I didn't lift my head again until the sun shone brightly overhead. I threw the rope ladder down and climbed to the *ground, falling from it when I was almost to the ground and landed with a thud. Half-asleep and scared the men might still be at the house, I stumbled and staggered over my feet until I reached the cottage, or what remained of it.*

No one was there. No bad men, no Daddy, and no cottage.

It was a blackened ruin as if it caught fire at some point during the night. I sank to the cold ground and cried and cried...

I shook my head and stared at the weed I'd mangled while the bad memories filled my mind. I hadn't seen that night so vividly in a long, long time. After seeing the house ruined, I'd wandered the woods until I found a road and followed it. Somehow, I managed to make it to this town. I'm not sure exactly how many days I spent wandering around until I found myself being stopped by a woman with a brood of kids around her.

Without my having to say a word, she scooped me up in her arms and took me home. After days of trying to track down my family with no results, since I refused to tell her my last name, she accepted me as another one of her kids.

I dropped the spade in the dirt and sank back on my butt.

Mama Lucy still didn't know my last name, and there were times I nearly forgot it. I repeated it aloud now, the sound of it weird even to my ears.

"Kate Darrah."

I said it three times before I felt comfortable in

the knowledge of who I was, or at least who I thought I was.

I tore off my work gloves and stared at the silver bangle in the morning sun. I outgrew it. It didn't fit on my upper arm anymore. Now it was on my wrist.

Dad said never to take it off. Never, but why not? He left me that night, left me alone in this world with his rules that got me nowhere. I had no mom and no dad. No family. I had nothing except this bangle.

He never gave me a reason to keep it on. Never told me why not to take it off. The runes meant nothing to me. Just weird designs I didn't understand, like the rest of my life before Mama Lucy found me.

Alone in the garden, I held my breath, and removed the bangle.

When nothing happened, I let out the breath I held and stared at the cold metal in my hand. The bangle was beautiful, but I didn't want it. I was a few months away from being eighteen, and when that time came, I wanted to leave Mama Lucy's house to start over.

I could bury it in the garden. No one would know. The idea sounded good, so I picked up the spade again and set to work digging a hole. The deeper I dug, the wider I grinned, feeling a weight start to lift from my shoulders—until a pain shot through my back and I gasped in pain.

The tension I woke with this morning was ten times worse, and I grimaced as the sharp pain spread through my shoulder blades and down my arms. But it wasn't normal pain.

I felt as if my body was on fire and something... something was moving inside of me, trying to get out. Trying to tear through my skin. I hunched over, alone in the garden, wondering if I was dying when I saw my bangle in the dirt.

Scrabbling for it, I slid it back over my hand and closed my eyes as the strange sensations instantly vanished. I blinked a few times, clearing away the disbelief of what happened and swore I saw the runes on the bangle glowing before it faded away.

I stretched my hand and my fingers, admiring the band in the sunlight, but it didn't glow again, and for those few moments, I doubted my sanity completely. Was I still dreaming?

"Kate! Mama Lucy says time for lessons," Mary said from the back door.

"Coming!" I replied, hearing my voice shake.

I picked up my gloves and the spade, and returned them to their place, wiping the dirt from my hands on my jeans. I was barely back inside the kitchen when Mama Lucy was there, eyeing me curiously.

"Kate? Something wrong?"

"Nothing I'm fine. Just something in my eye," I lied.

Her brow arched. "They look good to me. Are you sure it doesn't have to do with how you came to me?"

I hated when she did that, knew what I was thinking without my saying a word, or giving anything away. I stumbled over my words, and she draped her arm over my shoulders, leading me back outside.

"But lessons are starting."

"They can wait a few moments. That's the benefit of homeschooling."

I heard that line plenty of times before. On days it would snow, she'd let us all be outside to play in it, or when it rained and puddles formed in the backyard. Or any other time the weather was too nice, or too intense to be stuck staring at the pages in a book. She loved nature, and she instilled that same love in every kid she rescued off the streets.

We wandered outside to the greenhouse, but I stopped at the door.

"The plants will be fine. You're with me."

"Are you sure?" I fidgeted, remembering that lecture word for word about not rubbing off any negativity on the plants. "I don't want to kill anything."

She laughed, a deep sound that warmed me and made me smile. "Come along, Kate. You could use a good strong cup of tea this morning to chase away those nasty dreams you've been having."

"I never said my dreams were nasty," I mumbled as I followed her into the greenhouse.

It was humid like always, but comfortably so and the air smelled of fresh herbs that tickled my nose and instantly made me feel better. Whatever happened in the garden, it had to all be in my head.

Otherwise, it didn't make sense, and I had enough things in my past that didn't make sense to have any issues with the present.

Mama Lucy bustled around picking leaves from various pots and dropping them in the ancient stone bowl. "I wondered how long you would be able to keep them at bay on your own," she mused, watching me wander towards the crimson roses at the far end of the greenhouse.

"Keep what at bay?"

"Memories of whatever happened to you."

"Mama Lucy, I—"

She held up her hand to stop me, a gentle smile on her face. "You don't need to share with me. They are yours to keep, or yours to speak of when you're ready, if you ever are."

She turned the pestle, smashing down the herbs and mixing them together. I watched transfixed as she took a pot of water and heated it over a tiny Bunsen burner. When it was bubbling, she filled a metal steeper with the herbs, poured the water into a handless mug, and dunked them in.

"What will it do?" I asked as she handed it to me.

"Calm your mind and let you put your past behind you."

"I'll forget what happened?" I didn't want that, did I?

"No, child. It will merely clear your mind and let you sleep in peace. For weeks now, I've noticed a change in you. This will soothe you until you are ready to face whatever haunts you." She nodded, and I took a sip. "And remember, if you ever wish to speak with me, I'm right here."

I sighed as the warm tea slid down my throat and within seconds, did calm my racing thoughts. "I don't think you'll believe me," I whispered.

Just as quietly, I heard Mama Lucy reply, "You would be surprised what I know."

We stayed in the greenhouse until the tea was gone. She tended to the herbs I hadn't been able to, and when I felt ready to face the day, we headed back inside.

Everyone was at the table, ready for their lessons, talking or reading as they waited. When they saw Mama Lucy, they grinned, and I took my seat near the head of the table.

"Alright, kiddies," she said with a bright grin, "today we get to learn about the stars."

I settled into my advanced work, letting her lesson of the stars and constellations keep me grounded in this moment in time.

I was safe here with Mama Lucy, had been over nearly ten years.

I would be safe for another ten if I wished.

2

CRAIG

The security guard grunted, and I gently rested his head on the desk, careful not to make too much noise. I stared at the array of monitors before me and tapped in a few keys to create a loop in the system.

I scoffed again at my family's reluctance to learn all they could about humans and their technology instead of always relying on their magic to do the work for them.

Once the loop was in place, I had ten minutes to get into the exhibit, snatch what I came for, and get out again before the guard woke up.

The alarms were dismantled, and I was fairly certain there was no other staff on duty tonight. I watched the museum for two weeks, checking everyone's comings and goings so there would be no surprises.

I hated surprises. That I knew was the demon

side of me. My human half was more prone to showing emotion and giving in to my doubts about every plan I came up with. The curse I was stuck with for being Craig, the bastard son of Raghnall, Demon King.

The clan hated me from the moment I was born, saw me as weak and needing to be cast out, but Raghnall tried to raise me as his own and bring me up as he would any true-born demon son.

Too bad I was the only son ever born to Raghnall, which only made my situation that much more perilous.

But my human half always slowed me down and nearly killed me in my earlier years. I had to learn to adapt, to use my head more than my brawn, which I don't have anyway.

I taught himself magic that was forbidden for demons to know, and I found better ways of fighting.

Well, I wouldn't call them fighting methods really. I cheated, constantly, and I was damned good at it.

I smirked as I pulled the black mask over my face and crept from the security office into the depths of the museum. Exhibits of artifacts surrounded me, paintings and sculptures, but I wasn't here for art. There was only one item I wanted from this museum, and it was in the exhibit near the back of the first floor.

My head remained on a constant swivel as I moved from one room to the next, keeping a close eye on the time. Eight minutes left. I picked up the pace and rounded the corner to finally come face to face with what I was after.

"Hello, beautiful," I whispered.

The room was filled with weapons from across the globe and various eras. Humans assumed they were created by them, but the sword that was currently the star of the exhibit had not been crafted by any human hand.

Executioner.

That was the name of the long sword with its obsidian encrusted handle and rubies embedded in the hilt. The metal was darker than iron and much heavier, but a demon could easily hold such a blade without difficulty.

Centuries ago it was lost during one of the many great wars between demons and the other races. I spent the last year tracking it down for a buyer who was willing to pay me in more than just gold for finding it.

I didn't care about wealth. The buyer claimed to have an item that would lead me to my true prize, the only item that could aid me in the fight to come.

With only six minutes left of the loop for the security tapes, I hurried about my work, lifting off the glass case and removing the powerful relic of my kin.

I grunted as I hefted it over my shoulder and sensed the power running through it. Only a full-blood demon would benefit from it; for me, it was merely a means to an end. With the sword in hand, I exited the museum through the bay doors, the same way I entered earlier, with two minutes to spare.

Removing my mask, I sucked in a breath of fresh night air, chilly from being up in the mountains, and grinned at the sword.

"Another night and another prize."

I was meeting the buyer at midnight, in a park on the outskirts of the town. I unfolded the leather sheath tucked in the bag on my back, sheathed the sword carefully, and once it was safely hidden under my long, leather coat, I trudged towards the park.

A full moon lit my path, and I tried to keep my spirits high about tonight, but it was hard to do when I bore knowledge of what was out there. Not just out there tonight, but what was coming for me and all my kin.

No one listened to me. They thought I was crazy and maybe on some level I was. My own father cast me out when he caught me cheating my way through the trials that would have given me a much-cherished place in the palace, as I should've had anyway.

Instead, I'd been relegated to being nothing more than a foot soldier. It was a joke and a cruel one at that. The trials would've given me a mark at the end, telling any demon I met I was nothing important. That royal blood didn't run through my veins, when in fact it did. I cheated in my last fight against my opponent, used magic to curse his weapon so it would never hit me, and I'd been caught.

Raghnall had been furious, but I hadn't stuck around to deal with his wrath.

That was nearly four years ago. Since then, I'd been on my own, trying to study and understand the darkness spreading within the demon realm, but I sensed it would not remain there.

I reached the park a few minutes early and scoped out the empty playground and trees surrounding it. As far as I could tell, I was alone.

The heavy sword hurt my back, but I learned never to reveal an item until the buyer showed the payment agreed upon. At the beginning of my thieving career, I lost out on several deals. No longer.

Leaves crunched nearby, and the hair on the back of my neck stood on end. I sniffed the air, thankful I had slightly higher senses than a regular human, though not on par with a demon.

On the bright side, I didn't have to lug around horns all the time. I waited, hands tensed at my sides where my two daggers rested, words of power on my lips just in case, but the four beings that crept up, cloaked by the shadows were familiar figures, and I relaxed.

Slightly.

The temperature dropped as the four sorcerers stopped at the edge of the grass, unwilling to step onto the asphalt. Superstitious idiots really. I sighed and met them on the grass.

"It's not going to swallow you whole," I muttered under my breath.

The sorcerer with long grey hair down to his waist threw back his hood and glared at me, eyes blacker than the night sky overhead. "Careful, Craig. You may embrace humans and their technology, but do not expect us to."

"It's asphalt," I said, turning around to stare at it. "It's not really technology."

"Do you have the item or not?" he snapped.

"Depends if you brought what was promised or not," I countered patiently, crossing my arms and tapping my booted toe as if I had all night long for a standoff.

In reality, I was anxious as hell to snatch the damned thing from his robes and be gone. I needed to find a way to track down the only item that might be able to explain what was happening. A treasure lost in time, and nothing more than a rumor, until they contacted me.

The sorcerer's eyes darkened even more, and I sensed his power rising, but he reached into his robes and produced a broken piece of glass, colored, and with bits of a design etched on it.

"That's it?" I snapped, more of a growl as my anger rose. "Seriously?"

"It is what we promised."

"No, you said you would give me the item! Not a broken piece of crap!"

The sorcerer's hand moved before I realized it and was around my throat, squeezing. He didn't look strong, and in truth, he physically wasn't. But his power flared out and wrapped around my neck and slithered down my body, pinning my limbs together until I couldn't move.

He hissed in my face, and I cringed at the rotting stench coming from his mouth. I should've known better than to sink to dealing with these filthy men.

"Insult me again, boy, and it will be the last thing you do."

Just as suddenly as he grabbed me, he let go.

I managed to keep my feet as I choked and gasped for air. "Where's the rest of it?" I demanded as nicely as possible.

"We never claimed to have the entire piece. In fact, no one does. The pieces have been scattered. This is the piece we have held onto, and it is yours in exchange for the sword."

"And how am I supposed to find the other pieces?"

"With patience."

I glared at him fiercely, but he wasn't going to tell me anything else. Reluctantly, I started to reach behind my back for the sword when a new scent slammed into me, and I stopped.

"You let demons follow you here?" I hissed, whirling around in time to see them shimmering into view all over the park. "Great, that's just great."

"We did not bring them. Hand me the sword. We had a deal!"

"Well, well," a voice I never wanted to hear again

echoed across the park, and I cursed vividly under my breath. "Craig. Fancy seeing you here."

"Reginald." I stared at the six demons moving in behind him. "Do you often enjoy nightly strolls in random parks? I thought Raghnall would've kept you busy these days dealing with the other issues in our realm, or does he still not believe demons are disappearing."

"No demons have disappeared," he growled. "And you will address our king with respect the next time you speak of him."

I laughed. "Right, because he's always shown his son respect."

"You're not his true son. You're nothing more than a bastard... a bastard with a hefty price on his head," he added, and the demons moved in even closer, grinning darkly as one let manacles fall from his hands, the chains clinking together.

I swallowed hard even as I forced a grin to stay planted on my face. Couldn't show fear. That was a bad idea. "A price, huh? Placed on me by my own father. He should get a *Father of the Year* award."

I heard the sorcerers shuffling behind me before one of them snapped, "Our deal still stands. Hand me the sword, or you lose this piece forever."

"I'm a little busy at the moment. Can you just wait a bleeding second?" I responded over my shoulder. I didn't want to have to reveal the sword or use magic that would only piss them off more, but as Reginald stalked closer, I knew I was running out of options. "I need that glass shard."

"Then give us what we require!"

"What are you doing with those sorcerers?" Reginald was only a few yards away now, his black horns gleaming in the moonlight. He was tall and strong, the perfect demon and the son my father should've had. Too bad he was born to the king's younger brother and not him. He flashed his fangs at me with a grin. "I heard you sunk low these past few years, but I never imagined you'd sink this low."

"Not like I could turn to family for aid, cousin," I snarled.

Reginald technically had every right to be angry with me. He was the demon I fought in the last round of the trials, the one I cheated against and nearly killed when I lost control of the magic. He bore a scar from my blade that ran down the stretch of his chest. He'd been unable to defend himself, which I hadn't intended. Magic was tricky, and I'd been young and desperate.

Now I was merely desperate to get out of this situation with the glass shard and my head still firmly attached to my shoulders.

"Just come with us," Reginald said, but his voice was far from reassuring I would last longer than a few hours back home. "Father just wants you returned safely to us."

"And what, thrown in a cell for the rest of my days? I'll pass, thanks."

"I never said you had a choice in the matter."

My eyes darted around the park for an escape. Six demons. Six demons armed to the teeth who could easily overpower me... but not if they thought I wielded the Executioner and the power of the sorcerers behind me.

Knowing how badly this could go, I reached around my back and drew out the Executioner blade. It flashed before them as I whispered words of light under my breath, making the blade glow as if possessed by some incredible power.

Reginald flinched, but he didn't step away as I hoped. Hating to use more power in case this went really wrong and left me defenseless, I summoned fire and let it wash over the blade in vibrant, hungry flames. That got their attention and Reginald cursed as he realized what I held in my hands.

"Executioner... what are you doing with that?" he snarled.

"Using it, clearly," I stated. Now I had to get the shard and get out of there before I had to fight anyone with a blade I could barely hold in my hands.

"The sword," the sorcerer demanded behind me.

My hands fidgeted around the hilt as I watched Reginald's eyes narrow and he took a step back towards me.

Crap.

He wasn't buying it.

Time for plan B. From my pocket, I pulled smoke bombs that packed an extra kick and threw them down at my feet. Black smoke enveloped me and everyone in the park.

I lunged backward as they coughed and hacked, Reginald gasping and screaming for them to grab me. The sorcerers hadn't fled yet, and I reached out blindly, but luck was with me at least for a few seconds tonight.

I snatched the glass shard from the sorcerer's hands and took off across the parking lot.

"Where is he?" Reginald bellowed, and I ran faster. "Find him!"

"The sword! He took the sword!" the sorcerer screamed, but I knew they wouldn't follow, not if I stuck to the pavement.

The sword weighed me down, and I should've dropped it, but I could use it to sell to another interested buyer. I had to get away, get far enough away and cloak myself until Reginald and the rest of his hunting party gave up and went back home.

I hefted it over my shoulder, cringing every time it bounced and threatened to slice through my leather coat, but the smoke wouldn't last forever.

I turned off the main road and sprinted down a side road, not sure where it would lead. All I needed was a chance to hide, collect myself, and I could cloak my scent and my body from their senses.

Just a bit further—

"Gah!" I yelled at the pain blooming at my side and crumbled to the ground.

I reached around to find a dagger sticking out of

my body. Sucking in a deep breath and biting my lip to stop myself from yelling in pain again, I left it there and took off at a weird, sideways hobbling gait through the trees.

Reginald. I hated him, hated him for being the best damned hunter we had in our clan. Hated him for always wanting to take me down for simply being born.

My vision blurred, and I had to stop to catch my breath against a tree.

"Craig! Just stop running now, Craig, you'll only make it worse!"

I grunted at his words. I had no idea what would happen to me if I gave in and went back with him; no, I guess that wasn't entirely true. The darkness and plague spreading through our realm would continue to spread and kill everyone we knew because they'd lock me up, or kill me, and no one would try to stop it.

Ensuring the glass shard was safe in my coat, wrapped in a handkerchief, I pushed even deeper into the grove and sank to my knees.

"Craig!" Reginald's voice was closer now, and their heavy footsteps surrounded me.

I dug my hands into the ground and whispered the words for cloaking me from those who would wish to do me harm.

The wound at my side throbbed, and with every shift of my body, I felt the dagger still stuck in the wound. If I pulled it out now, I'd bleed everywhere, and that would draw them faster to me. I had to finish this spell... had to finish it... had to keep the shard safe...

I shook my head hard to try and stay focused on the spell. A rush of warmth burst from my hands into the ground, but I couldn't hold on any longer. Carrying that bloody sword around had worn me out, and I was tired, so tired.

The dagger in my side... they poisoned it. The thought hit me too late to stop the effects, and I slumped onto my stomach hitting the ground hard.

My breathing grew ragged, and the power that had enveloped the sword disappeared in a blink.

I was done for. They'd find me, drag me back to Raghnall, and all hope would be lost. I saw them emerge one by one from the trees around me, but when I glanced up to see Reginald's face, he looked right through me. The cloaking spell worked and so far, held up, despite my weakness.

"Where is he?" he seethed.

"The trail led here," one of the other demons pointed out.

"Then, where is he? Find him!"

"There are no footsteps to follow. He's gone."

Reginald snarled and slammed his fist into a tree, splintering the trunk and nearly snapping it in half. "Spread out. He couldn't have gone far. We are not returning to Raghnall without him."

I watched, holding my breath and struggling to stay conscious as they backed away from nearly stepping on me they were so close. Once they were out of sight, I let my mind go, unable to hold on any longer.

❦

SOMETHING WARM AND WET MOVED ACROSS MY FACE, and I jerked awake. A large bushy dog with black and white fur stared happily down at me, that warm tongue lolling out of the side of its mouth, its whole body wiggling as it wagged its tail.

"Thanks for that," I grumbled and sat up, pushing the dog away from my face.

It tried to get right back at me, plopping down in my lap and I realized my strange visitor was a he.

The dog barked loudly in my face, and I gave in, scratching behind his ears for a moment.

I turned and gasped in pain.

The dog leapt off my lap instantly and snuffled its huge snout around my side.

Gingerly, I reached around and then remembered what happened last night and why I was lying in the middle of the woods.

The dagger was still in my side, and blood oozed out around it. Bracing myself for the pain, I gave it a quick yank and flung several curses to the surrounding trees.

Birds took off for the sky at the sound of my ferocious growl as I dropped the blade and pushed aside my clothes to see the wound. It would take too long to heal for me to sit here. Reginald and his demons could come back at any time. I tore off a piece of my shirt and balled it up the best I could, pressed it against the wound, and used another piece to tie around my middle to hold it in place.

All the while, the dog watched, sitting and staring at me intently.

"What do you want, huh?" I asked grumpily. "I don't have any food. Go home."

The pain was bearable, no worse than any injury I'd had before, but Reginald had tainted the blade, and from the feel of it, it wasn't only a sleeping toxin. I was woozy and wanted to curl right back up and go to sleep, but there wasn't time.

I had one shard, one tiny shard of the object I hunted for. The sorcerers never even told me how many pieces there were. It could take years for me to track them all down, decades, and by that time, we'd all probably be dead. I needed help from the only race good at finding treasure.

And they hated demons, especially half-breeds of any kind.

"Bloody dragons," I whispered and tucked the glass shard back in my pocket. "Thanks for the wake-up, but I have to go now," I muttered to the dog.

He scratched at his ear as if he hadn't a care in the world about me going or staying. I tried to stand, but dizziness made me start to fall. The dog rushed forward and steadied me on my feet.

I could hardly stand without his massive body to keep me upright. And the sword was still on the ground. I wasn't about to leave it behind, so I took a shaky step over to pick it up and sheath it on my back.

I wasted nearly ten minutes, grunting and straining with my wound to get the sword back to its hidden location underneath my coat. Once it was there, I was out of breath and ready to sit back down and call it quits. But I had to get moving. Had to get out of these woods and figure out where I was going to find a dragon willing to help me.

In truth, I never understood why dragons didn't like us. I mean, not like my clan caused a war between the races nearly every decade for one reason or another. Not like we tried to assassinate their queen once, or twice... no check that, three times.

And now I was going to find one and ask him for help. Yeah, this was going to be a great day.

"Alright boy," I said as I stared at the dog following me. "Where are we? You hungry? We need some food... and a car."

He barked twice and set off at a happy pace through the trees.

I couldn't keep up, and he circled back more than once to try and nudge me along. He wore no collar, and I started throwing around names for the big beast of a dog whose head came nearly up to my chest. I was short by demon standards, but not my human ones. Whatever breed this guy was, he was a good thing to have by my side. If nothing else, he'd scare any curious people away.

The trees grew farther apart, and soon I found myself staring at a large town. Shops and houses were intermixed, but there were more pedestrians walking around the cars. Absently, I scratched the dog's big head and grinned when he turned his big ole brown eyes up to stare at me.

"Rufus, how about that for a name?" I asked.

The dog tilted his head and growled.

"Okay, no Rufus. Benji?"

He huffed this time.

"Harry?"

The dog seemed to think on that one for a moment before he barked and wagged his tail.

"Okay, Harry, it is. Now, where do we get some food?"

I was hesitant to step out into the open but standing at the edge of the trees would get me nowhere closer to solving the riddle of what hunted my clan.

Despite them denying anything terrible was happening, demons had been disappearing for years, and the few that returned were changed.

Sickness broke out constantly, and though I was no longer there to see it for myself, I had eyes and ears willing to keep me informed of the situation.

Harry bounded towards the sidewalk leading into town, and I hurried to follow, pressing a hand to my wounded side as it throbbed in pain.

The dizziness returned for a second and I cursed Reginald again for his antics. Just because I nearly killed him once, he felt the need to make my life miserable.

A café sat not too far into town. "Stay here," I told Harry, and he obediently plopped his butt down. "Weird dog. I'll bring you something."

Glancing around for any sign Reginald and his horde of hunters followed me, then ducked inside to grab some breakfast and figure out my next move.

3

KATE

Mama Lucy's tea failed to keep the nightmares away last night, and I had to get out of the house. Saturday was my day to wander the town anyway and do some running for Mama Lucy while I was out.

It was still early, and I'd skipped out on breakfast back at the mansion. Mama Lucy would've asked me questions, and I wasn't ready to tell her about my dream.

It started as they often did, me flying around high above the clouds... but this time... this time the sky turned black, and it started raining. But it wasn't water. It was worse, so much worse.

I shuddered thinking about it now and stared up at the clear blue sky overhead. No dark clouds here and no raining blood. The dream only got more horrifying from there, but I forced myself to think of something else as I headed towards the local café for some pancakes and OJ.

"Oh, hello," I said when I spied the large black and white dog sitting outside.

He barked and wagged his tail, headbutting me until I patted his head.

"No collar, huh? Are you lost, boy?"

I glanced around, looking for any sign of an owner, but there wasn't one around. He didn't look like he was in bad shape. His fur was soft, despite it being extremely bushy. His eyes were bright and alert, and he seemed happy.

"Are you hungry? How about I get you something to eat and then I'll take you home with me?"

The dog barked, and I grinned. I'd get my breakfast to go and lead him back to Mama Lucy. The kids would love to have a dog around for a while, and Mama Lucy never said we couldn't have a dog in the house.

I worried the furry beast would take off, but he circled twice and sank back down to the warm sidewalk, basking in the sun. I hurried inside and glanced around the café. It was busy with the usual faces, but I frowned to see a new one near the back corner. The town wasn't large by any means, and I was good at remembering faces.

The guy, maybe a year or two older, sat with his back ramrod straight and glared out the front window. His face was pale, and he hadn't touched a bite of the food in front of him. As I waited at the

counter to order, my gaze kept going back to him…
and for the strangest reason, I felt the urge to go talk
to him.

"Morning, Kate," Jimmy, the owner of the café
said as he neared my stool at the counter.

"Morning," I replied automatically, but barely
turned my head.

"Ah, I see. Busy checking out the new guy in
town?' he teased.

"What, no I just… is he alright?" I whispered.

As if the guy heard me, he stiffened, and his gaze
suddenly shot towards me.

"Not sure. Came in here this morning with that
dog outside. Barely said enough to order some food,"
Jimmy replied quietly. "Not sure I like the look of
him, so you stay away from him, alright?"

"What if he needs help?"

"Kate, what would Mama Lucy think, huh?"

I frowned.

He was right, but at the same time, Mama Lucy
taught us to look after each other in this town. He
was in this town, and he looked like he needed help.

"Can I get an order of pancakes to go, please?" I
ordered, even as I hopped off my stool.

Jimmy's brow furrowed, but he wrote up the
ticket and didn't say another word as I slowly made
my way towards the guy. The closer I came towards
him, the more I had to stop myself from rushing to
him and sliding into the booth across from him.
What was wrong with me? He was attractive sure,

with his sandy brown hair and its messy style and his piercing blue eyes, so pale they reminded me of ice in the winter.

"Can I help you?" he snapped.

I flinched.

I laughed nervously. "Sorry, I uh, I just haven't seen you around town before," I mumbled. "I usually remember everyone, but you're new. Passing through or coming to stay?"

His eyes narrowed, and I felt his annoyance hit me like a punch to the gut. "Why do you care?"

"Just curious is all."

I breathed deeply through my nose and froze. What was that delicious smell? It was magnificent and tantalizing... was it his food? No, Jimmy's pancakes never smelled so good. Like all the holiday dinners mixed together.

I breathed again, and he tilted his head, watching me. I stopped sniffing the air, realizing what I was doing and that I probably looked like a crazy person. "Sorry, it's been a weird morning."

"Sure," he said.

"Right, well, I just didn't know if you needed help or something." I watched him closely, but then my gaze shifted to the item resting against the seat beside him. It was wrapped in leather, but the light refracted off of something red and sparkling beneath it.

My shoulders tensed and the sensation of something trying to move beneath my skin had me stepping back quickly.

"Are you this weird around everyone you meet?" he asked annoyed.

"Uh, no... no... what is that?" I blurted out, pointing to the thing.

His hand automatically went to it, and he glared at me. "None of your business, little girl."

"Little girl?" I snapped and fiddled with the silver bangle on my wrist. "Seriously? I'm just trying to be nice, and you're going to bite my head off?"

"You haven't exactly been nice."

"I was worried about you. You look like someone's chasing you," I pointed out. "All I was going to say was if you needed help, I know someone you would be safe with."

He glanced around as if I'd brought in a team of other people to corner him. "Who sent you?"

"What? No one," I muttered. "I came in to get breakfast for me and that dog, but then I was told that dog is yours so just getting food for myself."

"Harry, his name is Harry," he grunted as if I offended him by not knowing the dog's name.

"Maybe you should get a collar for your dog," I shot back.

"That's none of your business."

"You're right, totally right."

It took another second to take in his weird look, the long leather trench coat, and the torn-up shirt beneath, and his pants. They weren't jeans. He was wearing knee-high leather boots, and... were those breeches?

"Did you come from a convention?"

"Now you're going to insult what I'm wearing? You're great at making new friends, aren't you?"

My hands curled into fists at my sides, and the strangest urge to smack him across the face hit me. I stopped myself short and backed away.

"You know what, never mind. I didn't want to help you or your dog anyway. Crazy, paranoid freak," I mumbled and stalked away.

I paid for my pancakes and grumbled as I stepped outside. I gave Harry a long scratch behind the ears and stomped down the sidewalk. I'd eat my breakfast in the small park then do my running for Mama Lucy.

That guy, he was such an asshole. All I tried to do was help. My steps slowed, and I frowned realizing he might have been right. I had acted weirdly. I'd been sniffing the air like a dog. And that thing with him, what had it done to me? A shiver shot down my spine as flashes of my dream last night hit me again.

Didn't matter. I'd never see him again. I'd do my running, go home, and try to catch up on some sleep and pray that whatever strange crap was going on with me was nothing more than a fluke.

4

CRAIG

I left a twenty on the table, picked up the wrapped sword, and without touching anything on my plate, or waiting for change, headed out of the café. I'd pocketed a pancake for Harry at least, and he gobbled it up as soon as I offered it to him.

"Who is she?" I whispered to him, watching the weird girl walk down the sidewalk.

At first, I thought she was some townie who was going to hit on me. Happened before, but then she'd been sniffing the air. Sniffing it, intently, and I'd watched as her gaze zeroed in on the sword. The idea crossed my mind she was a witch of some kind, sent after me by Reginald, but she was a piss poor one if that was the case. No witch was that clumsy.

And then I saw the bracelet on her arm.

She was no witch, not even close. She was exactly

who I needed, and she was storming off through town.

I patted my leg and Harry fell into step beside me. I carried the sword over my shoulder, keeping my eyes trained on that head of black hair. The conversation replayed over and over in my head, and each time, I found another thing that made me curious about who she was. Her eyes were intense as she'd spoken to me, but at the same time, she seemed so unsure of herself. What was someone like her doing in this tiny town anyway? As far as I knew, there were none in these parts. They rarely frequented the human realm, not wanting to risk exposure.

Many centuries ago it happened, and it was disastrous for their kind. They were still rebuilding, and yet one of their own was out here wandering the streets of some mountain town in Colorado.

The runes on that bracelet were old, older than many I'd seen before on one like her. She had no guards following her that I could see. Was it possible she was really on her own? My luck might be holding out, and I picked up the pace.

When she'd sniffed the air, I thought at first, she was being weird, but now I realized if she was what I thought she was, then the glass shard in my pocket had been what she smelled. I couldn't lose her. She might be my only chance to track down the rest of the shards.

The girl turned off the sidewalk, and my gut dropped thinking I lost her, but then Harry barked and took off through the small crowd, and I caught the end of his bushy tail disappearing into a small park.

I couldn't run and hoped he would slow her down. Warmth spread from the wound at my side, and I knew it opened up. I healed slower thanks to my human half, but usually, it didn't take this long. And never before had I needed stitches to aid in the closing of a wound.

Whenever I saw Reginald again, I'd have to pay him back in kind.

Harry's barking guided me through the tiny park where a small playground was set off to the side, and a few art pieces were displayed, popping out here and there amongst the bushes. I clutched at my side, grimacing as the pain grew and my feet staggered.

"Hi again," I heard the girl say, laughing at the dog. "Where's your mean old owner, huh?"

I tried to call out, but the words stuck in my throat. I collapsed to the ground, coughing and hacking as a chill spread through my bones. What the hell was this?

"Hello?" the girl called out. No one else was in the park that I could hear. Harry barked and a few seconds later, I saw his furry feet before my eyes.

"Oh God!" The girl was there, grabbing my arm and trying to pull me to my feet. "You idiot!"

"Idiot?" I managed to rasp, trying to get to my feet with her help—and the dog's.

"Yes, idiot. I asked if you needed help and you chased me off by being an asshole," she snapped.

Her anger made me grin, and I tried to laugh, not exactly sure what was funny about this situation. I might be dying, but all I could do was laugh.

"Come on, we're getting you to a hospital."

"No," I growled, and she stiffened, but didn't run off. "No hospital."

"What's wrong with you anyway?"

I couldn't find the words again and pointed to my side. She shoved away my shirt and gasped.

"That's a lot of blood. Okay, I'm taking you to my place. Can you walk?"

"Where... where is your place?"

"Not far, but there's a woman there, she can help you."

A woman? I needed to know who, or what, but my mind became a muddled mess. My arm draped over her shoulders, and she started to lead me away, but the leather-wrapped sword was on the ground.

"Wait!"

"What?"

I nodded to the sword on the ground. "Can't... can't leave it."

"Seriously? You could be dying, and you're worried about that thing?"

"Priorities," I mumbled, and she glared at me. I removed my arm and Harry helped me stay standing as she bent to pick it up. I was about to apologize for it being so heavy, worried she might not be able to carry it around, but she hoisted it easily into her arms, and then put my arm back around her shoulders. "Who the hell are you?"

"That's not very nice to ask the person helping you."

I winced with every step we took back down the park trail and out to the sidewalk. She held me up and carried that sword as if we weighed nothing. If I doubted what she was a few seconds ago, I didn't any longer.

But the question remained if she knew what she was.

I guess I'd have no choice, but to let her take me back to this woman and hope it wasn't a trap.

⚜

"WHAT IS THIS PLACE?" I GRUNTED WHEN WE FINALLY reached a huge old, mansion smack dab in the middle of town. "You live here?'

"Yes, now I told you to stop talking and save your strength," she scolded.

I grinned. "I'm fine, perfectly fine."

She glanced worriedly at my side, and I knew that was clearly not the case. "You should've just let me take you to a hospital," she muttered.

"No hospitals," I growled again, but weaker, much weaker. "They don't do well treating patients like me."

"Oh, you mean stubborn jackasses?"

"You're funny you know that?" I squinted at her as my vision blurred. "And kind of cute when you're mad."

She opened her mouth to say something else, but I didn't hear it. It was like someone put cotton in my ears and my legs gave out, too.

I crashed to the ground, and Harry started licking my face.

I tried to lift a hand to pet him, but it didn't reach.

All I could do was lay there, on a stone path, and stare up at the sky.

5

KATE

"Idiot!" I snapped again as I rushed up the front steps and into the house. "Mama Lucy!"

"Kate, what's the matter?" she asked, rushing out of the kitchen.

A few of the kids followed, but one look at the panic on my face and she sent them back outside to play.

"Kate?'

I grabbed her hand and dragged her outside with me. "He needs your help."

Mama Lucy's face darkened the second they landed on the guy. "Where did you find him? What happened?"

"At the café," I rasped as she ran to his side and knelt down.

Harry promptly sat back on his butt watching contently.

"I tried to talk to him, but he was being rude, and

then he followed me, and I saw the blood, but he said no hospital."

"Take a breath, Kate," Mama Lucy ordered gently. "Help me get him inside."

"No hospital?" I asked confused.

"No, not for this. Come on."

She grabbed his feet, and I hefted him up at the shoulders. Together, we managed to get him up the few wooden steps, and inside the living room with pocket doors she slid closed.

Then she was back at his side as he laid on the couch, peeling back his coat and lifted his shirt. The wound looked awful, not that I'd seen many wounds before in my life… or none, really.

"Is it supposed to look like that? All weird and oozing?"

"No. Whatever stabbed him was poisoned."

"Stabbed? Poisoned?" I stared intently at the guy's face. "What's going on? Why would someone stab him?"

Something pawed at the door, and I rushed to open it thinking it would be one of the kids, but it was Harry, dragging that huge sword behind him by the hilt.

I picked it up for him, and he trotted to sit by the guy's head. I leaned the sword against the wall, more concerned with him surviving than the trinket he had with him. Who walked around with a sword anyway?

"Kate, I need you to grab me a few things from the

shop," Mama Lucy said, poking and prodding around the wound with her fingers.

I gagged and turned away, not wanting to see what was happening to the wound.

"Grab a pen and paper, it's going to be quite a few items."

I nodded and rushed out of the room to find a paper and pen. I peeked out back, but all the kids were still out there playing and laughing in the garden, safe and sound and not seeing that ghastly wound.

I ran back to Mama Lucy and jotted down everything she told me.

"What is this stuff?" I asked, staring at the list. "I'm not sure they sell this at the pharmacy."

"You're not going to the pharmacy," she informed me, her brow crinkled so deep I wondered if it would un-crinkle. "He needs different help besides the medicine of men."

I blinked a few times before muttering, "What? That doesn't make sense."

"I know, but I have no time to explain right now." She removed a gold coin from the pocket of her skirt, and my eyes went straight to it.

The urge to snatch it out of her hands grew in me suddenly. I forced myself to back away.

"I need you to go to the herbalist shop three blocks over, you know the one."

"I've never gone there before. You said I wasn't

allowed to," I whispered, my still eyes transfixed by that gold coin in her hand.

"And now I'm telling you to go there. Take this," she said and grabbed my hand, setting the coin in my palm.

It was heavy, not physically, but I couldn't describe what it did to me. I rolled my shoulders and broke out in a cold sweat.

"Kate, look at me."

The power in those words made my eyes whip to her, and I shook my head. "Sorry, right, the shop."

"Give this coin to the woman behind the counter along with the list. She'll give you what you need. And hurry. Your friend doesn't have much time."

I tucked the coin into my front pocket and nodded. "He better be nice to me after this," I muttered and stomped for the door.

The guy grunted in his unconscious state, but it came out more of a growl. His lips moved, and he mumbled a few words I couldn't make out, but then Mama Lucy was shoving me towards the door.

"Is this his dog?" she asked, nodding to Harry sitting by the couch.

"I think so, at least he said it was. I'll be back as soon as I can."

The wound oozed more blood as we'd stood there talking and not wanting to waste any more time, I darted out of the house, and sprinted through the streets.

My mind raced with possibilities of what was going on, but each one was crazier than the last. The guy had been stabbed by someone and carried around a sword, had a weird dog as a companion, and growled.

None of it made sense, but then again, nothing about these past few days made sense. The dreams had gotten worse, and the sensation that I was not alone in my own body intensified at random times throughout the day.

I took a deep breath as I rounded the corner and took off again. A tantalizing scent made me come to a dead stop.

The coin.

My eyes darted to my pocket, and I placed my hand over it. I wanted the coin, wanted to hold it again and keep it... but I couldn't.

"What is wrong with me?" I picked up the pace and turned my thoughts back to the guy on Mama Lucy's couch potentially going to die if I didn't get back to them both fast enough.

Whatever else was going on, the only thing that mattered was not letting that rude person die on the couch. I had a feeling he'd come back to haunt me one way or another and never let me forget I failed him.

I was maybe a block away from the shop when I turned another corner and slammed right into a group of people.

I took one of them down with me as I yelped in

alarm, but somehow, he managed to twist us mid-fall, and I landed on top of his hard, muscled form.

"Oh God! I'm so sorry," I gasped, but the rest of the words stuck in my throat.

He smiled, and it lit up his face, his very smooth, chiseled face. Two bright blue eyes met mine, and I swore they glimmered.

"That's quite alright. Are you hurt?"

"Am I hurt?" I repeated dumbly and shook my head. "No, I'm fine. How did you do that?"

"Do what?"

"I was going to land on the sidewalk, and then you moved, and I crushed you."

"I hardly call this crushing me, and you seem to be enjoying it since you have yet to move… though your elbow is digging into my ribcage."

I yanked it away and tried to get off his very comfortable, very warm chest. "Sorry! I'm so sorry."

He helped me, and I noticed his buddies standing close by, staring curiously at me. "It's alright. Not every day a beautiful woman runs into me."

"Yeah well, I'm in a hurry and crap! I'm sorry, I have to go!"

I took off at a run again, but a glance over my shoulder told me the guy stood there with a mix of confusion and delight on his face as he watched me go.

Damn it! Why couldn't I have just stayed a few seconds longer? Gotten his number maybe? But that was selfish of me. The other guy I ran into was about to die if I didn't hurry. There was no time for getting numbers from handsome guys on the street.

And I didn't know either of their names.

Fantastic.

But that second guy, he seemed familiar. I hadn't seen him around town before, just like the first one, but he was different.

I wrinkled my nose as the notion that he *smelled* familiar passed through my mind. How could someone smell familiar? Was it his cologne maybe? But I was lying right on top of him, and I was pretty sure there was no cologne on that guy anywhere.

He looked a little older, too. Maybe nineteen or twenty. College guy. Could've been in town for something I guess. I shouldn't know who he was, but that voice in the back of my mind said I did and I should turn back to find him again.

"No," I told myself firmly and sprinted the rest of the way to the shop. "Have to save the idiot first."

Outside the shop with windows filled with herbs and oils, candles and hanging charms and ornaments, I waited a few seconds longer, to catch my breath, then sweaty and a bit out of sorts, stepped inside the one shop I'd always wanted to go into, holding my breath for what I might finally get to see.

A bell chimed over the door as I entered and a strong, familiar scent that reminded me immediately of Mama Lucy's greenhouse hit me hard. Soft flute music played from speakers in the ceiling, and a bubbling fountain filled the center of the shop.

The walls were lined from floor to ceiling and filled with jars and bottles, wooden boxes, and things with names I couldn't even pronounce. More glittering charms hung from the ceiling.

I glanced up at them as I moved slowly through the shop. There was one wall dedicated to books and another to horns and other strange looking items that had to be for show.

"May I help you?" a voice came from behind me.

I turned to see a woman with jet black hair and piercing ice blue eyes standing behind the counter. She had a broom in one hand and a red shawl around her shoulders.

"Yeah, sorry, Mama Lucy sent me," I said, gulping down my apprehension over being here.

But the woman's face softened immediately, and she smiled, waving me forward. "Well then, welcome. You must be Kate."

I frowned. "How did you know?"

She nodded her head towards my wrist and the bangle. "I know many things, child, and I know your time is precious. Why have you come? Where is Lucy?"

I couldn't speak for a moment but remembered the wound on that guy's side and rushed to pull the coin and list from my pocket. "She's helping someone. Said we needed the things on the list and to pay you with this coin." I handed both of them over, though my fingers tried to cling a moment longer to the gold coin.

She whispered over the list. "My, my, this is interesting. Wait here. I'll gather what you need."

As she disappeared into the back, I meandered around the shop to keep my mind from thinking the worst. If I was too late… if I couldn't get back to the house in time…

No, I was going to think positive. I might not have known that strange guy for long, but I could tell he was a fighter. He'd live. I knew he would.

I glanced aimlessly around the shop as I walked but stopped when voices whispered as if people stood right beside me, speaking into my ear.

I whipped around, but I was alone. The voices were still there, but when I moved towards the counter, they grew quieter. Curious, I took another few steps towards the far corner of the shop, and they increased. I winced at how loud they became when I reached a small table, and everything fell deathly silent.

Sitting on the table was an intricate looking dagger, gold hilt encrusted with sapphires. It was the most beautiful thing I'd ever seen. Dragons were etched into the sheath around the blade and even the hilt curved into the tail of one.

I reached out to touch it and like a magnet, my hand tightened around it. The shop fell away, and I was no longer a girl in a shop.

I soared high above the town, heavy wings beating the air as I pushed myself higher and higher above the clouds. When I rose above them, I was free.

Finally, free!

Wind rushed past me, and I rolled as I soared effortlessly through the air.

Then the sky darkened and turned red, and screams came from below.

I flew below the clouds, and the town was gone.

Instead, a castle stood in its place surrounded by other buildings on fire. People screamed and ran, but from what, I couldn't see.

A massive body flew right by me, and I stared in awe at another great beast like me... and another... and another. The sky was filled with dragons, fire shooting from their mouths as they attacked the shadowy force overwhelming the land, but it did nothing to hold it back.

I tried to flee, but I was no longer in control. A roar erupted from my great body, and the dragons rallied to my side.

As one, we flew towards the shadow. I opened my jaws, my inner fire shot upward, through my throat...

"Kate," a stern voice snapped, and my hand was yanked away from the dagger.

"What... sorry... what was that?" I asked panicking as I staggered away from the table.

"I said to wait by the counter." She didn't sound angry; concerned, but not angry.

"Sorry, yeah." I sheepishly shoved my hands in my pocket and stepped back to the counter.

"I'll have your items ready in a few minutes. I

recommend you not touch anything else. You might not like what you see."

She disappeared into the back of the shop again leaving me to wonder what she meant... and what the hell I'd just seen.

6

CRAIG

"That does hurt you know," I growled as fingers poked around the wound again.

"Stop being a baby," the woman muttered and pushed harder.

I winced and bit the inside of my cheek, so I wouldn't snarl and snap my jaws at her. "Who are you?"

"Lucy. I'm the witch who's trying to save your life."

I sat up long enough to stare at her smirking at me mischievously, and then sank back to the couch. "Damned witches. I knew that girl was trouble. Damn it!"

"Oh, quit your whining. Kate has nothing to do with our kind, yours or mine."

"Kate, that's her name?"

"Yes, the girl who saved you from dying on the street like a dog." She dabbed at my wound with a clean cloth and met my gaze. "And you are a half-demon. Why are you here? And why are you carrying around that behemoth of a sword?"

I wasn't about to tell my life's story to a witch I didn't know. "It's a long story."

"We have a few moments, and I think I have a right to know since you're running around with my daughter."

"Your what?" I sat up at that and studied her face. "She's not really your daughter, she can't be."

"Adoptive daughter," she corrected. "But still mine to protect."

"Are you in the business of protecting dragon shifters?"

Her gaze turned dangerous in a heartbeat, and her hand hovered over my wound as we stared each other down.

"If you try to harm her, I will let you lie here and die. Do you understand me, demon? I have no love for your kind."

"No one does, but are you going to condemn me for the crap my kin does?" I lowered my gaze to the wound. "That was inflicted on me by my cousin because I'm a half-breed bastard son. My father put a bounty on my head. Dying here on your couch is preferable to being dragged back there so let me die if you like." I closed my eyes and settled into the cushions, waiting for her to make her next move.

She blew out an aggravated breath and dabbed gently at the wound again. "You can at least be honest with the witch trying to save you. Who are you, truly?"

"Exactly who I said. My name is Craig."

"Raghnall's son?" she asked in alarm. "The demon king's son?"

"Bastard son, remember?"

"And you have that blade with you, why? Are you planning on killing your father?"

"Ha, if only killing the demon king was that easy," I replied, not sure if I meant it or not. Could I kill my father? He was a downright ass and obviously wanted to lock me away to rot for the rest of my days, but he was still my father. "No, I was trying to trade it."

"That is a very important relic of the demon race, and you were simply going to trade it away? For what?"

How much could he trust this witch? "Something important."

"And that's all you're going to tell me?"

"I was stabbed by my own kin. I'm not really in the trusting business."

"Hmm, and yet you trusted Kate enough to let her help you. Why?"

I clenched my jaw and remained silent.

"Obviously you're in danger, and you are potentially endangering myself and those I care about by being here. I could throw you out on the streets, but I'm not. You know why?"

"Out of the goodness of your heart?" I mocked.

"No, because Kate asked for my help because she saw something in you. She trusts you," she pointed out. "She brought you here without question."

It was true; where I came from if someone found me bleeding and close to death, they would've left me where I laid and taken anything valuable I had on me. Kate risked her life to get me somewhere safe. She might not have known she risked her life, but she did it all the same.

"Does she know she's a shifter?" I asked quietly and noticed the witch stiffen. "That bracelet on her wrist, I saw those runes for entrapment."

"Kate's story is not an easy one," she whispered sadly. "Even I don't know all of it."

"So that's a no."

"It's safer that way," the witch said, but didn't sound convinced.

"Is it? She won't be able to suppress who she is forever. Either she'll figure it out, or something will happen to make it come out of her."

"You don't think I know that?" she snapped and stood, pacing back and forth. "Something's changed in the world. I can feel it, but whatever it is, it's preventing me from seeing too far. There's too much darkness and shadow, but the nagging in my mind tells me it's only the beginning."

"You've seen it?" I asked surprised.

She turned to stare at me. "You know what it is?"

"No, but I've seen what it does. Demons in my world, they're getting sick, dying. My father doesn't believe we have anything to worry about. It's why I left. Well," I added, "part of the reason why I left."

I winced as the wound throbbed and my vision blurred. damned Reginald and his poisoned blade.

"My story's not an easy one either, I'm afraid."

She glanced towards the windows. "Kate should be back soon. You only have to hold on a while longer. The salve I'll make will pull out the poison and heal you faster. You'll be fine in a few hours."

"I'm not sure I have a few hours," I said honestly. "I'm actually surprised they haven't shown up here."

She grinned and pointed to the charms hanging in the window. "You think I would leave my home unprotected?"

"But I'm in here?"

"Because I allowed you to be. Couldn't very well have you dying on my front lawn."

I managed a smile through the grimace of pain. "You know, she might not be your real daughter, but I can see where she gets her mouth from."

I thought I heard her laugh, but the room spun around me, and I clung to consciousness. I focused on Kate's face, wanting to see it again when she returned. She had to know the truth of who she was, if only so I could convince her to help me. I needed a dragon shifter to track down the rest of the pieces. If she could track them down, there would be a chance to stop this darkness from taking over the realms because it wouldn't stop there. It would spread to the human world, too, and they would be powerless to stop it.

Harry growled, and his snout stood straight up as he sniffed the air.

"What's he doing?" the witch asked.

"I don't know. He found me this morning passed out in the woods."

"He's not yours?"

"No, but he's been following me around. What is it, Harry?" I asked, growing weaker by the second.

He sniffed the air again, and his growl grew fiercer as he turned to the window, got to his feet, and stalked over, hackles raised. Something was out there.

"Harry?"

But then it hit me, and I sat up too fast. The room spun, and I was nearly sick.

"Stop before you hurt yourself more," the witch scolded, rushing to keep me upright.

"Kate, where is she?"

"Why, what's wrong?"

"They're here. I can sense them," I gasped, and tried to stand, but my legs gave out. "Have to help her."

"You can't go anywhere right now. She'll be fine."

But she wouldn't be fine. Reginald. He and his demons, they were out there, and they weren't the only ones. Dragon shifters, a number of them were close. Too close. I tried to stand again, but the witch forced me back to the couch, and I was too weak to push back.

All I could think of was Reginald going after Kate, hurting her and me unable to do anything but lie on this couch and wait for him to make it to me. This witch might think she could keep out demons, but she wouldn't be able to keep them out forever. They'd find a way in, and when they did, I wouldn't' be the only one they went after.

Harry kept watch at the front window with the witch at his side. I wondered why the dragons were here. I hadn't sensed them earlier when I was out with Kate. I glanced at the sword, the one I could barely lift. If they came here, I'd fight them the best I could.

No one was taking me back to Raghnall easily. Wound or no wound, I was not going down willingly or easily.

❧ 7 ❧

FORREST

I watched from across the street as the strange girl walked around the shop. She'd slammed right into me and hadn't even realized what I was.

She'd been in a hurry, and after I told the others to move on ahead without me, I followed her to spy her disappearing into that witch's shop. Taking up a place across the street, I waited intently to see where she would go next in such a hurry.

What fascinated me most was she had a very interesting scent about her. She was dragon kind, that I had no doubt of, but there was something else. Human and the reek of demon. I wanted to ask her what she was doing with a demon, but she'd run off before I had the chance.

More worrisome was why I was here in this town, to begin with.

Word went out a few mornings ago of a bounty

on the bastard son of Raghnall. I'm usually not into collecting bounties, but orders are orders, so I took my team and here we were in this town searching for the half-demon, trying to find him before anyone else did.

It wasn't the bounty's gold I cared about, well not truly. A dragon always coveted treasure. What was more important was the truce his capture might finally bring between the demons and dragons. For too long our clans fought and killed each other for reasons none of us even remembered.

The door to the shop opened, and the curious girl stepped out. She was like me and yet she wasn't. I spotted a flash of silver and gold at her wrist, and my nostrils flared in anger.

Someone kept her trapped from expressing her true form. She couldn't be the dragon she was meant to be while wearing that horrid thing. She appeared in distress as she tucked the paper sack under her arm and raced down the sidewalk again.

Not wanting to lose her, I hurried after, keeping my distance just so I wouldn't freak her out and she disappeared completely. She ran a few blocks over and then came to a large, wooden house surrounded by a fence and protective spells.

I snarled as I was forced to come to a stop before I was thrown backward. The girl raced up the steps and into the house without fail, but I knew I couldn't do the same.

"Who are you?" I whispered growing annoyed at my inability to understand this riddle.

I had to see inside the house but couldn't get too close. Otherwise, I risked giving myself away. If the protective spells around the house allowed her to pass, perhaps they would do the same for me simply because of what we shared.

The power pulsing from the house was strong, but when I breathed in deep, I realized I'd found more than just the home of this mysterious young woman.

My eyes narrowed.

There you are.

The bastard half-demon. He was here.

Was he responsible for keeping her trapped with that bracelet? All I knew of him was his thieving track record. He stole relics from all races and pawned them or sold them off for his own gain. He was a traitor to all races, not just the demons. It would be a pleasure to stop him from bringing any more harm to our kind. I stalked around the house as I texted my brethren to tell them our target had been found.

When I reached the rear of the house, I heard children playing and I paused. I couldn't let innocents be harmed. The demons might be fine with barreling in without a care for who might get hurt, but dragons were above such ruthless tactics. Dragons were placed here to protect, not destroy, unless absolutely necessary.

I would wait as long as I could, but before this day was over, I would have the half-demon in chains, and the bracelet torn from that poor girl's wrist. She needed to be freed.

And I would make whoever placed that bracelet on her pay for their heinous crimes.

8

KATE

I was still shaken up by what I saw in the shop but handed over the supplies to Mama Lucy the second I was through the doors to the living room.

She took them and went to work, mixing and mashing ingredients together in a bowl on the coffee table.

"You... made it back," a gruff voice said from the couch.

The guy was pale, very pale.

I sank to the ground by his side and held his hand, not sure why I did it, but he attempted a smile. "Yeah, I did. You have to hang in there. Can't die on Mama Lucy's couch, that'd be rude."

"Trying... not to... poison makes it... hard, you know?" He tried to laugh, but it turned into a hacking cough.

I shushed him. "I never caught your name."

"Craig," he whispered. "Name's Craig, and you're Kate."

Mama Lucy must've told him. "Yeah, that's me. The girl who saved the crazy guy."

"Did you... did you see anyone else... out there?"

Huh?

"That's quite enough talk," Mama Lucy said firmly and came over with the bowl filled with a foul-smelling salve.

I breathed through my mouth, but then I tasted it and gagged.

Mama Lucy's smile was grim. "It's potent, I know, but it'll work."

Craig swallowed hard and sucked in a pained breath when she pressed the thick, grey substance to his wound. I let him squeeze my hand, confused by his last question. I saw people out there, but I sensed he meant something else. Maybe the person who stabbed him?

"Craig, what did you mean?" I asked, earning a scowl from Mama Lucy.

"He needs rest," she said.

"She needs... to know..." Craig gasped when she pressed more salve into the wound. "Has to know."

"What's he talking about?"

"Nothing, he's delirious."

"No, I'm not," he growled.

This time I knew it was a growl. A beast-like growl that no human should be able to make.

Mama Lucy's hands stilled, and I froze, heart, pounding as I stared at him.

Panic was in his paranoid gaze as it flickered past me to the window. "They're coming... for me... I sense them... she needs to know the truth."

Mama Lucy opened her mouth probably to yell at him some more, but I cut her off. "Are you saying the person that did this to you is out there? Mama Lucy, we have to call the cops."

"No more humans," he rasped. "They'll only get hurt."

"Humans? We're all humans," I replied confused. "Craig?" He closed his eyes, and they didn't open again, but his chest rose and fell with his breathing. "What's he talking about? What do I need to know?"

"It's from the wound, dear, ignore it," she said.

I shook my head. "Mama Lucy, what's going on? Really? I know things have changed. Something's happening, and I have no idea what it is and at the shop..." I trailed off, unsure if I should tell her what happened at the shop or not.

"Kate?" Her hand held my cheek as she stared deeply into my eyes. "What did you see?"

"There... there was a dagger, and I touched it, and then I wasn't here anymore," I whispered. "I was flying... I was a dragon, and there was fighting. People dying." I gulped at the fear and anger racing through my veins. "And a darkness spreading over everything. Killing everything. I tried to fight it, but then... then I was back in the shop as if nothing happened. It was like my dreams only this felt… this felt real."

Now I sounded like a crazy person. That was just great. But when I looked at Mama Lucy, she wasn't staring at me like I was crazy.

She stared at me like she already knew this day would come. "Oh, my sweet girl, maybe he's right."

"Told you," Craig chimed in followed by a harsh cough.

Mama Lucy glared at him. "She has to be told the proper way. Not just blurting out the truth!"

"No time… can't you… feel it? They're here… running out of time."

"No one is getting into this house!"

I glanced from one to the other and wondered if I was the only sane one in this room. "Would someone please just tell me what's going on?" I snapped and felt the strange sensation of something shifting through my body as if trying to break through my skin again.

There was no pain like the other day when I tried to take off my bracelet. No, this was different. This felt powerful and strong, and I closed my eyes, ready to embrace it when Mama Lucy grabbed my shoulders hard and the sensation died.

"Not here, you can't do that here," she ordered. "Never, do you hear me?"

"I don't understand! What's happening to me and who is he?" I was ready to tear my hair out if no one came clean.

Harry's sharp bark interrupted our arguing.

Mama Lucy let go of me and ran to the window. Her face paled, and she backed away. "Kate, get the kids. Lock them in a room upstairs."

"What? Mama Lucy—"

"Do as I say!" she stormed.

I bolted from the room, stopped for a second to peer outside and saw someone I never expected to see again.

The guy I ran into on the street was there along with the guys I assumed were his friends.

But there were more guys headed towards them and from the looks on their faces, they weren't happy. Why were they all here?

"Kate!"

"Right," I muttered and ran through the house to the backyard. "I need you all to come inside, come on!"

"What, why?" Jerry, one of the younger boys, asked. "I don't want to go in."

"Mama Lucy says so, now hurry up. It's an emergency." I waved, urging them all inside.

They groaned complaints as they came inside, and I hurried to lock the back door. I counted heads, making sure I had everyone, and ushered them towards the stairs.

"What's going on, Kate?" Mary asked.

I was about to make up some lie when a horrible roar came from outside. It shook the walls, and the kids shrieked in fear.

Mama Lucy yelled something I didn't understand, and then the sound of glass shattering had me moving faster than I ever had before in my life. Leading the way, I took the kids upstairs as sounds of fighting erupted at the front of the house. All I could think of was Mama Lucy staring down those men and yelled for the kids to move faster. I had to get them to safety before I could go help her.

"Inside," I said and opened the door to Mama Lucy's room. "Now you lock this door, and you don't open it for anyone except me or Mama Lucy, understand?"

"Wait, where are you going?" Mary asked, grabbing my hand. "What's happening?"

"I don't know, but you're going to stay in here. I have to go help."

"No! Don't leave us!"

I stared at all the faces and wished I could tell them everything was going to be alright, but how could I do that when I had no idea if it would be or not?

"Keep this door locked," I repeated and closed it. I waited until I heard the bolt slide into place then rushed off back downstairs to help.

But downstairs was chaos.

A guy I didn't recognize went sailing down the hall, past the stairs, and landed with a thud somewhere in the kitchen. He yelled curses from his tone, but what he actually said I have no idea. The language was weird and very guttural.

I heard Mama Lucy yell and I took off in the direction it came from.

When I skidded around the corner to the living room, Mama Lucy was backed up against the far wall, her hands out before her and blue and white light emanating from them. It formed a bubble around her and kept out the men trying to get at her.

"Mama Lucy!" I screamed and without thinking about the consequences, barreled into the men invading my home.

I took them to the floor in a heap, but once there had no idea what to do next.

"Kate!" Craig yelled in a panic.

I turned to see him using the sword he'd been carrying and fighting against another man with a sword.

No, not just a strange man.

The other man I ran into on the street! Why was everyone running around with swords?

"Grab her!" the man I ran into earlier ordered and a strong pair of arms wrapped around me, pinning my arms to my side.

"Get off me! Let me go!" I screamed, but the one holding me was too strong.

"Forrest! The demons are back," one of the others I'd knocked down said, staring out the front window. "And they do not look happy!"

Forrest, the man attacking Craig, the one I'd knocked down in town, snarled and pressed harder with his sword against a still weak Craig.

Craig sank to one knee, and I caught his eye.

I urged him to get up and keep fighting!

I had no idea who he really was or what the hell was going on, but I was not going to watch the guy I spent all morning trying to save be stabbed to death in my living room!

"Get the portal open," Forrest ordered.

"No! You're not taking her," Mama Lucy screamed, and more light shot from her hands.

My jaw dropped, but there was little time to stand around being shocked by what I was seeing.

The man near the window was blasted through the glass to land on the front lawn, but another rushed in to take his place.

Craig suddenly sprang up from the floor, whirling the blade faster as he went on the offensive.

I kicked and flailed, trying to break loose.

The guy's arm moved closer to my mouth, and I bit down hard until he finally let go with a snarl.

Forrest spotted me falling to the floor and opened his mouth to yell, but I picked up the closest item I could find, a brass bookend, and chucked it at him.

He ducked, and it thudded into the wall instead.

"We're trying to help you!" he bellowed at me.

Craig scoffed, swinging the sword wide.

Forrest's blade caught it just in time from slashing into his side.

"Then why are you attacking her? Kate! You have to get out of here!"

"She'd be safer with us, demon," Forrest snapped.

"Demon?" I repeated and screamed in annoyance. "Would someone please tell me what the hell is going on!"

Forrest looked as if he was about to do just that when the guy I bit slammed his open palm into the nearest wall.

He'd used his blood to draw symbols around where his hand was, and the sheetrock crumbled away.

"Demons are coming! We have to go, now!" the man yelled.

Mama Lucy was back on her feet, and light bloomed in her palms. "I've had enough of this!" she snapped, but it wasn't Mama Lucy's voice anymore.

This, this was different, powerful, and it slammed into me, nearly sending me off my feet.

She raised her hands towards the glowing hole in the wall.

Craig ducked under Forrest's blade and lunged towards me, taking me to the floor just as Mama Lucy let loose.

The power shot towards the portal, but instead of closing it, which I think was what she tried to do.

It exploded outward.

The man who stood before it was sucked in and a moment later, Forrest followed.

Craig started to go, and I held onto his hands, struggling to keep him there, but his grip slipped.

"Kate!" Mama Lucy screamed and rushed forward.

We couldn't hold on.

Craig cursed as he was dragged into the swirling light and my fingers grazed Mama Lucy's as I was sucked in after him.

"Mama Lucy!"

Her face filled with fear right before the room was filled with more strangers and then everything was gone.

I fell and fell, screaming as I tumbled head over heels before finally, I landed with a thud on something hard and the world around me went dark.

9

CRAIG

Everything hurt, again. I blinked, trying to make sense of where I was when a blade appeared at my throat.

The dragon shifter who attacked me at the house stood over me, smoke slipping from his nose as he glared at me with those glowing eyes.

"What did you do?" he snarled.

"Me? I'm pretty sure it was the witch who messed up your portal," I said sounding calm. I mentally applauded myself for not losing it yet. "Where are we?"

"I don't know, but it's not home." He held is sword against me.

"Clearly." I tried to move, and the blade pressed in harder against my skin. "Is this really necessary? You know I can't blink, right? Half-demon, means I only get a few of the benefits of a full-blooded demon."

He narrowed his gaze at me, but pulled the blade back far enough so I could sit up. "Jenson isn't here."

"Who?" I asked, brushing dirt and muck from my sleeves.

"Jensen, one of the guards with me. He came through first, but I don't see him."

"Did we all land in the same area?" I glanced around suddenly frantic. "Kate! Kate, answer me!"

The blade appeared at my throat again. "You are not to go near her."

Angry now, I shoved his hand away and clambered to my feet. "And why the hell not? I met her before you did and all you did was make a mess of her home."

"That was the home of a witch keeping her trapped," Forrest argued hotly and put the blade back for a third time. He stared me down as I glanced from it to him and laughed. "You think this is funny?"

"I think your face is funny," I said lightly. "But this? No. Now if you'll excuse me, I'd like to find Kate before something else does. Kate!" I yelled again and ignoring him and his blade, hoping I was calling his bluff that he wasn't going to kill me, started off in a random direction to find Kate.

After a few feet of walking, I found the sword and picked it up. Forrest went on guard immediately, but I didn't care about some stuck-up dragon snob right then and kept walking.

The lighting was dimmed, but not completely dark, and the foliage was strange. Everything had a tinge of grey or black to it, like it was sick. Or dying. I stopped abruptly and spun around in a circle.

"What's wrong?" Forrest asked, immediately pressing his back to mine.

"You know, for acting like you hate me, you sure are trusting me to protect your ass," I muttered.

"I don't know where we are, or what dangers are out there. I can put my hatred aside if it means we survive. Besides," he added, "I don't want to kill you."

"Huh, I find that hard to believe."

"I don't. That would go against my orders."

"And let me guess," I mumbled, squinting into the shadowy half-dead looking forest around us, "you always follow your orders perfectly. I think I hate you more than you hate me now."

"At least I'm honest and not a lying, stealing, cheating—"

"Yeah, I got it." I looked around us again, and up into what bit of the sky I could see. "Damn."

"What? Is there something out there trying to get us, or not?"

I lowered the sword to my shoulder and turned to face him. "Yeah, there's going to be lots of things trying to get us, so I suggest we be quiet and try to find Kate and this Jensen of yours."

He didn't sheath this blade, but he didn't point it at me either. We were making progress.

I turned back and walked quieter, searching for any sign of where Kate might have fallen. I did not want her waking up to this dark world all alone and taking off in a panic. She'd get herself killed in seconds.

Though to be honest, I hadn't expected her to be so courageous during that fight at the house. She might not know she was a dragon shifter, but she had the characteristics of one. The good ones, not the stuck up holier than though attitude like the one walking beside me.

"Your name is Forrest, right?" I asked as we walked.

"Forrest, son of Kadin of the Chimalus Clan."

I groaned, annoyed. "Of course, you're a bloody prince."

"What's that supposed to mean? So are you."

"No, I'm not, as you seem to already know since you and your friends were after me for the bounty, too. Why else would you be following me around?"

"I didn't follow you," he said. "I followed the girl."

"Kate?" I asked hotly. "What do you want with Kate?"

"I should be asking you the same question," he snapped. "Why is a half-demon running around with a dragon shifter? Are you the one that trapped her in her current form?"

"What? No."

He sighed heavily. "So, it was the witch then."

"Wow, are you always like this?"

"Like what? Protecting my kin? Yes."

I laughed, forgetting for a moment we were supposed to be quiet. I couldn't help it. "Oh man, no I mean running into situations and assuming the worst of everyone before you know what's going on?"

He flinched as if I'd hit him. "I saw quite clearly what was going on," he started, and I walked off. "Where are you going?"

"To find Kate, but please continue. I'd love to hear what you were going to say."

"That bracelet on her wrist. Someone cursed her."

"Not even close." I put my arm out to stop him when I heard rustling coming from our right followed by a groan. "I think she's over here." I moved towards the sounds, and Forrest kept talking.

"She should be with her own kind."

"That witch you're so ready to punish has been keeping Kate safe for a very long time."

"You know this for sure?" he asked surprised.

I shrugged. "I'm guessing from what I saw."

"No, a witch would not raise a dragon. She couldn't, not the way we're meant to be trained."

More rustling. I stopped again and crouched down when a large, shadowy shape separated from the trees ahead of us.

Forrest sank down beside me without a word. The guy might sound like a bloody fool, but at least he knew how to pay attention.

I pressed a finger to my lips and crept closer.

He grabbed my arm to stop me, but I tugged away from him.

Kate was close, I knew it somehow.

And that thing, whatever it was, might be going for her.

We couldn't let that happen. Together, we sifted through the underbrush, but staying quiet was difficult. Everything was dead, and it creaked and cracked with each move we made.

I cringed every time, expecting the beast to turn around and come after us, but it stayed on its course. The great hulking thing was close to ten feet tall, if not taller, some bear-like creature. If we were where I thought we were, I prayed I was wrong about what I was seeing.

"Are you sure she's over here?" Forrest whispered a few tense minutes later.

I was about to agree with him, that maybe my instincts were wrong after all when a high-pitched scream tore through the silence.

"Kate!"

I sprinted through the trees, no longer trying to be quiet. Brandishing the sword, I burst through the trees to see the large beast hoisting a flailing and screaming Kate into the air.

It stood over ten feet tall easily, fur blacker than night and thick covering a hide I bet was even thicker. Fangs dripping saliva hung over its bottom lip, and the talons currently holding Kate were a few feet long and stained dark, probably with the blood of its previous kills.

The beast held her in one hand easily, claws extending from its massive hands, and when it whirled around on us, jaw wide open, fangs dripping with saliva and blood were there to meet us.

The beast growled ferociously, but I didn't stop my charge.

Hefting the sword high, I attacked, aiming to slice it open, but it swatted me aside like I was a bug.

"Craig!"

I groaned in pain and watched Forrest lunge forward next with quick jabs at the creature, but his blade barely broke the skin.

I found my feet and told Kate to hold on.

She yelled something back, but I missed it as I attacked the beast with Forrest, but no matter how hard we hit it, nothing penetrated its thick hide.

"What are you waiting for?" I finally snapped, running out of strength from repeatedly lifting the sword. "Burn it!"

Forrest threw his sword down, and I backed away as he thrust his chest forward with a bellow that turned into a roar. His body shifted and grew in size, changing from that of a man into the coiled form of a blue-scaled dragon with eyes of ice and wings that flared out behind him. His massive body barely fit beneath the trees, but he didn't need to move. All he had to do was light the beast on fire.

"Kate! Cover your face," I ordered, and I saw her duck down at the last second as Forrest's jaw dropped and flames shot out from deep within his glowing chest.

The beast screeched in pain as its fur lit up and he

dropped Kate to the ground. She curled up in a tight ball, protecting her head and stayed there even after the beast took off into the forest as a flaming, living torch.

When Forrest clamped his jaws shut and swung his heavy head around to stare at me, I grinned in approval. Dragons were handy to have on hand. Fire killed most things.

I rushed over to Kate and fell to my knees beside her.

"Kate, it's over. You can look now. Come on, are you alright?"

Slowly, her arms fell away, and she lifted her head to stare at me and then past me to where Forrest's massive dragon form was shrinking back down again.

I helped her to a sitting position and smiled, waiting for her to tell me she was fine, but then she scrambled away, eyes wide with fear.

"Would someone please tell me what the hell is going on? Right now, and I mean right now. Did he just change into a dragon? And someone said they were a demon... and Mama Lucy, what was Mama Lucy doing!" she ranted, pacing back and forth in a tight circle. "And the light... and falling, I don't understand what's going on. Any of it!"

I held up my hands to try and stop her, but she backed away again.

"Alright, just calm down. We'll explain everything. Just take a breath before you pass out."

"Don't patronize me!"

"I'm not," I assured her as Forrest slowly walked over to join us. "Take a deep breath."

"I don't want to take a deep breath," she seethed, and I saw the dragon shifting in her eyes. She rolled her shoulders and her neck as the change rippled across her body, but she never shifted. The bangle on her wrist glowed faintly for a few seconds before it faded away. "I just want some answers."

A loud howl made us all jump, and I gripped my sword in my hand. "How about we find somewhere a bit safer to talk first? I think our friend's coming back—"

More howls joined the first. "And he's bringing friends," Forrest muttered.

I spun in a circle and looked around.

A stone outcropping that rose high above the trees. "Who's ready for some climbing?" I asked happily.

Neither found me amusing.

I nodded. "Right, let's get out of here and then we'll talk."

"damned right we'll talk," Kate muttered as she fell into step behind me.

I smiled despite the horrible situation we found ourselves in.

Maybe being thrown through a portal wouldn't be as terrible as I first assumed.

❧ 10 ❧

FORREST

I glanced up at the sky. "Does the sun not rise here?"

"Nope, never," Craig replied. "It used to, a long time ago."

"That's if you know where we actually are," I stated. "And you could be wrong, which means we would have no idea where we are or how to get back."

He poked a stick into the tiny fire I'd created to keep the chill away.

Kate sat near the fire, but well away from both of us, staring intently into the flames. She hadn't said a word since we decided to take Craig's suggestion and climb up here.

I hated to admit it, but it'd been a good one. The beast had come back, singed fur and all, with four more, but they hadn't been able to climb up and get us.

My father always said even the tiny victories were worth celebrating. I counted this as a very tiny victory since we were currently trapped in an unknown world with dangerous creatures and I was unsure if Craig was going to try and kill me or not.

"Why don't you just open up another portal and get us back?" Craig suggested. "Like the other guy did."

"It's not that easy to make a portal." I refused to meet his gaze when it narrowed on my face.

"Seemed pretty easy to me."

"Well, it's not. We'll just have to find another way."

He barked a laugh, pointing the charred stick at me. "I knew it! You're weaker here, aren't you."

I lifted one shoulder. "I was able to shift, that's what matters."

"But you weren't able to use your magic, so we're screwed. Stuck in The Burnt World until we find our way home except... oh wait," he announced brightly, "there is no way home!"

I rolled my eyes. "if there's a way here, then there's a way to get out of here."

"Not how it works, at least not with this place."

"That doesn't make sense! We landed her, didn't we?"

"Because the witch's magic interfered with another portal," he explained. "It created a pocket for us to slip into, but unless we recreate it all exactly the same way, I doubt we'll get back the way we came in."

I was good at fighting, always had been, but magic

and spells were beyond my skill set. That was the reason I had Jensen around. I needed to find him, get a portal open, and take Craig to my father. And Kate, too. Kate who should have been with her kin since birth, but wasn't.

"Seriously?"

I flinched at Craig's abruptness. "What?"

"You're already plotting against me, I can see it in your eyes. Can we worry about surviving first?"

"I said I wasn't going to kill you."

"That makes me feel loads better."

I held my hand to the flames, and they washed over my fingers. "It should."

A strange sound came from Kate's side of the fire, and we both turned, confused. Her head was lowered, and she shook uncontrollably.

I worried she was having a fit of some kind, maybe this Burnt World as Craig called it was affecting the bracelet and her ability to change.

But when she lifted her head, her cheeks were flushed, and she burst out laughing hysterically. She laughed so hard, she cried, holding her sides as she rolled backward into the dirt.

Craig and I exchanged a concerned look as she kept it up, not close to stopping anytime soon.

"Ah, Kate?" Craig tried, but she only laughed louder.

"I fail to see what's so funny," I said, and she sat up, wiping the tears from her face.

"What's so funny," she said in between gasping for

air and more bouts of giggles as if she were a child, "is that you're apparently a demon of some kind and you," she said, pointing at me and laughing harder. "You're a dragon! You changed into a dragon right in front of me!"

I stiffened. "I still fail to see the humor here."

"And then," she went on as if I hadn't spoken, "then I find out Mama Lucy, who I thought was a witch, is actually a freaking witch! With powers, real powers! And we get sucked through a portal to land in this... this dark, terrifying place where apparently monsters really exist too! This, this is hysterical!" She was back to laughing as if she'd heard the funniest story in the world.

Craig grinned and chuckled with her, but there was nothing about our current predicament that was funny at all. "You two are insane," I stated.

"Yes, yes, I'd have to be to believe this was all real," Kate agreed. "That's it, I've completely lost my mind, and this is all in my head."

"No, it's not, and you need to pull yourself together," I snarled, tired of her attitude.

She might be a dragon on the inside, but this was not how we reacted to situations. We did not have mental breakdowns and laugh in the face of such dire circumstances.

"Forrest, come on, give her a break," Craig said. "This is a lot to take in."

"We need her focused. How do you think we're

going to get out of this mess if she can't keep herself together for five minutes?"

Her laughter slowly quieted as she turned from me to Craig. "Please tell me I'm really crazy?"

"You're not crazy," I said as Craig said, "Maybe a little."

We glared at each other.

"No, then that would mean… at the house, all of that actually happened?" she whispered, and all humor died from her face. Finally.

"Yes, it did—"

She threw herself at me over the fire, and we rolled back into the bushes.

"You asshole! What did I ever do to you?" She drew back her fist and punched me right in the nose before I could react. "You hurt Mama Lucy! And the kids! There were kids in that house!"

She tried to hit me again as Craig sat by and watched with glee.

"A little help," I muttered as I dodged another hit and tried to catch her hands. "Craig!"

"Sorry, think you deserve this."

"damned straight he does!" She tried to hit me again.

I managed to throw her off and pushed to my feet.

"You could've hurt those kids and Mama Lucy! If your guys hurt her before I get back, I'll kill you!"

"Those guys weren't all mine. Ask Craig."

She blinked once then twice and turned to face

Craig, holding up his hands as she stalked towards him next, while I stood by and watched.

"Now hold on just a second," he said, struggling to find his feet and back away before she could hit him next. "They were only there because they followed Forrest. Mama Lucy said it herself, they couldn't track me once I was inside the house because of the charms."

Kate drew back her fist anyway, and I had to hand it to Craig, he took the hit like a champ, letting her deck him twice before he swiped out his foot and she fell to the ground with an oomph. Her arms flung out to her sides, and she just laid there, staring up at the sky.

"All of it happened," she whispered, and we both nodded. "Will they hurt Mama Lucy and the kids?"

Craig's shoulders sagged, and for the first time since meeting him face to face, I felt sorry for him. Slightly.

Craig made a half grimace. "Mama Lucy seemed pretty powerful. I don't think my cousin and his hunters will stand much of a chance for long against her."

"You're really good at not answering questions," she mumbled, still on the ground.

I walked over and held out my hand for hers. She eyed it warily, but Craig did the same, and together, we pulled her to her feet.

"I thought you knew," I said and frowned when Craig started shaking his head frantically.

"Knew what?"

"Knew about our world, about what I was because of what you are."

Craig groaned and turned away, hands clasped behind his head.

"And what am I?" Kate asked sharply. "An idiot for trusting him and for not realizing the man I ran into on the street was dangerous?"

"No, because you're a dragon, too."

Kate's jaw dropped, and she stepped backward as a strangled sound escaped her mouth. She clasped the bracelet on her wrist, mumbled something about the dreams being real and then keeled over a second later.

Craig managed to catch her before I could and cradled her head on his leg.

"Nice going," he growled. "She didn't know what she was."

"How could she not know?"

"It's a long story." He gave her a little shake, but she didn't wake. "Right. I'll take first watch. Get some rest. When she wakes up, I'll wake you."

"Or we both stay watch." I sat down with my back to the fire and faced the trees surrounding us.

A foreboding feeling sank into my gut as Craig whispered, "Whatever you say, scale-boy."

I rolled my eyes at his words and focused on my task, pondering all the while how someone could grow up and not realize a beast lived within them.

11

KATE

I didn't have to look up to know Craig and Forrest were exchanging another look. When I'd opened my eyes a few minutes ago, I'd been staring right up into Craig's face. He'd sighed with relief to see me awake, but the last thing I wanted was to have my head resting in some... some demon's lap.

Demon. I couldn't believe I thought that right now.

Demons and dragons.

"Kate," Craig started, but I held up my hand, and I saw his mouth shut.

I poked the fire with a stick, picturing it was both of them. I hadn't really meant to go off on them earlier. I told myself all those times I felt something living inside me that I was making it up and it was all in my head. But now, now I knew it was a lie.

I fiddled with the bangle at my wrist, tempted to

remove it, but what would happen then? I lost my temper without taking the bangle off, and I feared what I'd do if I really let my true self show. My dragon self.

"Okay. I want to ask some questions, but we're going to use simple answers."

"Simple answers?" Forrest repeated. "I'm not sure how that will work."

"It'll work by you guys not over-complicating matters," I muttered. "Yes or no answers and very short explanations. I'm still trying to accept the fact that I'm a... I'm a dragon." Wow, that sounded worse out loud than it did in my head. "First question, where are we?"

Forrest held up his hands, and I turned to Craig for an answer.

"Can we start with an easier question?" he pleaded.

"It can't be that hard," I argued, but his face told me otherwise. "Alright, we'll come back to that one. Who are you?"

"Who or what?"

I stabbed my stick into the dirt hard, and he smirked.

"You're really going to sit there and smile at me?"

"Sorry, you're cute when you're angry."

"Craig, remember that I saved your ass today," I reminded him through gritted teeth.

"True. I am Craig, son of Raghnall, Demon King, and ruler of Boshen."

"King?" Damn, and here I thought this question would be an easy one to start with. "Okay, so you're a prince? And Boshen, I'm almost afraid to ask, but I'm assuming that place is not where I'm from."

"Technically I'm a prince, but a bastard one. My mum was not exactly a demon."

"What was she?" I asked, hoping I wasn't going to regret the answer.

"Human. And Boshen is not in your world. All of our homes have been removed from the human world in an effort to keep us safe," Craig explained, using his hands I guess to help his words. "Essentially, there are portals to get to our worlds, portals that should only be opened with the utmost care." He threw a glare at Forrest across the fire.

"We would have been fine if a spell hadn't been cast careening us off course," he growled.

When they looked ready to argue again, I angrily stoked the fire, and they fell silent. "You can tear each other apart later. Now, what and who are you?" I pointed my half-burnt stick towards Forrest.

He bowed his head as he formally introduced himself. "I am Forrest, son of Kadin, chieftain of the Chimalus clan."

"So not a prince?" I clarified.

He shrugged. "Depends on who you ask, but I am of royal descent."

"Guess it could be worse, stranded out here with two princes." I poked at the ground again, head whirling, but I was doing my level best to stay calm and not have another freak-out. I could tell Forrest didn't approve of me going off on him, or my blacking out afterward, but this was a hell of a lot to take in. I was a dragon. Or at least that's what he told me. How could he know? And Craig, did he know, too? What had he and Mama Lucy talked about while I was gone?

And Mama Lucy. She was a real witch.

All of this was too much. I wanted to go home and go back to my quiet town and my quiet life. There had to be a way to just get out of here and leave them here to fight it out. I stood and took three steps until I remembered that giant monster that attacked me and I promptly turned around and sat back down.

"So, you really don't know what you are?" Forrest asked quietly as if worried I'd deck him again.

"No, I didn't know, and I still don't think I believe you."

"How can you not after what you've seen?" he shot back. "Honestly, you're a dragon. The faster you accept that, the faster we can find a way out of this mess, and you can return to where you belong."

Craig sucked in a breath as he muttered, "Wrong move, man."

I felt something shift within me again, rolling my shoulders as the sensation to let free my anger again nearly had me ripping off the bracelet to finally see what would happen. "What did you say?"

"You're a dragon. Your place is with me and the rest of your kind."

"And who the hell are you to make that decision for me?"

"I am technically your prince," he said.

Craig shook his head frantically.

"I think someone disagrees with you," I said, nodding towards Craig.

Forrest's nostrils flared, and smoke poured out of them. "You know nothing."

"Actually, I do. I paid attention when I was being raised in my father's house, and I know a dragon only owes allegiance to the chieftain that rules each clan and the families within it. Unless her family is part of your clan, she does not have to do as you order," Craig said with a smug smile and crossed his arms. "You're welcome," he added to me in an undertone.

"She doesn't know which family she comes from, do you?" Forrest asked as he turned towards me. "That bracelet, who gave it to you?"

Self-conscious, I spun the bracelet around and around on my wrist. "I don't want to talk about it," I whispered, remembering how vividly I saw the events of that night the other day in the garden. I was not about to share those details with these two idiots. Not unless I had to.

"Then how are we supposed to help you?"

I glowered at Forrest and opened my mouth to tell him exactly how he could help me when a growl slipped from my lips.

Startled, I slapped my hand over my mouth as Forrest blinked at me and Craig scooted back a bit.

"What was that?" I whispered when I thought it might be safe to talk.

"That was your inner dragon," Forrest told me. "If you allow me, I can help you control it."

"But that would mean letting it out, right? Taking the bracelet off?"

"It's the only way, yes."

"Then no, not right now. I think we should focus on getting back home."

"No," Forrest said impatiently. "I am returning you both to my home. Craig has a bounty on his head and you, you do not belong in the human world."

"I belong with Mama Lucy and those kids!"

"And I bet that witch is the reason you've been trapped all your life!" He was on his feet as he ranted, more smoke trailing from his nose as his fingers curled at his sides. "There is a reason we do not associate with that kind!"

I was on my feet next, ready to go for round two, but Craig stepped in between us, stopping me from doing something I'd probably regret later.

"Leave it be for now, alright? Kate's right. Our main focus should be getting out of this realm."

I backed away a few steps and held my hands up to show I wasn't going to go after him. "Works for me as long as it's the human world."

Did I really just say that? The human world? It didn't matter. Later, when we were safe, and I was back with Mama Lucy, I'd let myself fall apart completely and laugh hysterically at what had happened to me.

"If I knew where we were, I might be of more help," Forrest commented.

Craig scratched the back of his head. "Look, I'm just guessing. I could be wrong."

"A guess is better than running around blind," I sighed. "Just spit it out, where do you think we are?" There, see? I could sound perfectly calm and collected when I wanted to.

"You called this the Burnt World when we arrived," Forrest said. "I've never heard of such a place."

"And you wouldn't, not if you didn't dig around for some lore on the plague."

"Plague?" I repeated. "What plague?"

But Forrest was already laughing, well not laughing really. More of a mocking cackle that made me want to smack him. "There were rumors floating around that you'd completely lost it, and I see now the rumors are true. A plague? You speak nonsense."

"I speak the truth that no one wants to believe." He threw up his arms as he spun in a circle. "Look around you? What do you think is killing this world, huh? I can tell you it wasn't always like this."

"And this plague killed the world?" I asked trying to follow.

"No," Forrest growled. "There is no plague. He's lying."

"Why would I lie? Why? I gain nothing from lying about a plague that's going to kill us all. Why does no one want to believe this is happening?"

"I want to believe you, but I'm having enough issues accepting dragons and demons are real."

Craig walked over to the nearest tree and using the sword he carried, swung it wide and sliced off a branch. It fell to the ground with a loud thud, and I glanced around worriedly. Those giant furry beasts couldn't be too far behind, and any loud noises could drag them over here. Including my yelling from earlier. I'd have to be more careful.

"What are you doing?" Forrest demanded. "We don't have time for show and tell."

Craig ignored him and picked up the branch. He motioned for us to come closer to look at the branch. Forrest mumbled something about half-demons being prone to madness, but when I moved forward, so did Forrest.

"You can't tell me that doesn't worry you at all," Craig muttered.

I leaned in to stare where the rings of the branch should've been visible. But instead, a strange almost metallic black ooze filled the branch. It stank of rot, and when I reached closer, it bubbled and started to churn.

"What's it doing?" I asked, transfixed by what I was seeing.

His mouth moved, but whatever came out was lost on me. The dark ooze called to me. I reached out to touch it, wanting to see what it would do when a high-pitched scream reverberated through my mind.

I smashed my hands over my ears, trying to block it out as something warm oozed out of my ears. I sank to my knees, begging for it to stop, and then it cut off violently.

"Kate! Kate, can you hear me?"

I opened my eyes to find Craig looking down at me, brow creased in worry, but it was the fear in his eyes that told me what I just experienced was not supposed to happen. "I'm alright," I muttered.

"Your ears are bleeding."

"Really?" I lifted my hands to them and cursed when they came away bloody. "That's awesome. Just add that to the list of crappy things happening today."

"Uh, guys?" Forrest muttered, but Craig was too busy pulling me to my feet and checking my eyes.

He was close, very close, and I had a chance to catch the woodsy scent on him. I liked it, but then gave myself a hard shake. We were in some plague-stricken world with monsters wandering around. Now was not the time to focus on how attractive this half-demon was.

"Craig!"

"What?" he snarled, and I saw his face darken as his demon half looked ready to come out to play. I had no idea what he would look like if that happened and frankly, wasn't sure I could handle that on top of everything else.

"What is that?"

Then I glanced up and realized Craig shifting would be the least of my troubles.

"Run," Craig gasped, taking hold of my hand and sheathing the sword at his back. "Run!"

The black ooze slipped from the branch and as I chanced a look over my shoulder, saw it rise up and form into a beastly figure with arms way too long to be human and legs that bent backward.

Its head reared back, and a horrifying scream escaped its lips. I'd been letting Craig pull me along, but now, I sprinted with everything I had as the thing gave chase.

12

CRAIG

If I made it out of this damned world alive, I'd start taking a poll about why it took so long for people to believe me when I tried to tell them something that could save their lives.

The plague spawn screeched again, and the ground trembled beneath my feet.

"How do we kill it?" Forrest yelled as he raced on beside us.

"Fire!" I called back.

"Why didn't you say so?" Forrest slid to a stop, and I almost sent Kate and me flying as I brought us to a sudden stop.

"No! Not dragon fire—you idiot!" I hollered as he shifted on the spot.

"You said fire," Kate panted as she tried to catch her breath.

I shook my head. "It's immune to dragon fire if the dumbass would've stopped for two seconds and listened to me!" I bellowed. "Did you hear that? Your fire won't work!"

"I don't think he's listening to you."

"I realize that."

I watched as Forrest finished shifting, placing himself between us and the plague spawn. It wouldn't be able to kill him easily, but I was more worried about him getting infected somehow and then bringing it back to us. It wasn't that easy to catch the plague, but I was guessing. I'd only been able to study small samples of the plague before I was banished from the demon world. The creature raced closer, and Forrest spread his wings wide, his chest glowing as the embers deep in his chest lit and made ready to fire.

"That's not going to work!" I yelled again, but he was either pointedly ignoring me, or just couldn't hear me. I'm pretty sure it was the first option.

"What's going to happen if that thing gets him?" Kate asked.

"I'm not sure, but I doubt it'll be good."

"If his fire can't kill it then what fire can?" she asked, eyes wide with fear.

"Fire blessed with the potion I swiped from a witch."

She glared at me, and I shrugged.

"Not from Mama Lucy, was it?"

"No, this came from a horrible old lady who was about to keel over and die. Not like she was going to use it anytime soon."

"Seriously?"

"What? Desperate times, love." I watched as the plague spawn reared back on its hind legs to challenge Forrest. I needed to get a torch, drop some of the potion on it, and then light the thing on fire, but right now, that seemed impossible. "We need to keep running."

"Maybe his fire will kill it," she suggested as Forrest opened his mouth and let loose.

I doubted it, but I held my breath and prayed she was right all the same.

The gods, however, were not that kind.

The fire overwhelmed the beast, and by all rights, it should've been nothing, but a pile of goo again. But when Forrest ran out of steam and closed his mouth, the plague spawn was still there.

And now it was pissed off.

It lunged towards Forrest, and he struggled to take off in the low hanging branches and trees so close together. His wings couldn't extend, and the spawn latched onto his back, tearing into his scales.

Kate moved before I even had a chance to. She took off with a yell, and no weapon.

At least I didn't think she had a weapon, but that girl's hands were better than mine.

I never felt her grab for the sword, but she wielded it now, high over her head as a growl tore from her mouth. I sensed she had no idea what she was doing, but her dragon instinct kicked in to save one of her own.

Figures.

And now I couldn't just run away to leave Forrest to fend for himself. Cursing, I took off after her, not sure of my plan yet.

The spawn had already torn away several scales by the time Kate reached it. She leapt into the air with inhuman strength and brought the sword slamming down on the spawn.

It shrieked in rage and threw its body back, taking her with it to the ground. Forrest staggered forward, trying to shift back to his human form as I joined Kate in trying to keep the thing contained.

I rushed towards it, but it opened its mouth and black ooze issued forth, spilling, bubbling like acid on the ground at my feet.

"Don't let it get on you!" I warned Kate as she found her feet. "Do you even know how to use a sword?"

"Doesn't matter does it!" she shot back. "Find a damned torch or something!"

"Why is it," I demanded hotly as I searched around for a branch that might not be infected, "that every single dragon I meet is bossy?"

I found one on the ground, weathered and brittle, but no sign of the plague poisoning it. I tore a bit of fabric from my shirt, wrapped it around and dug in my pockets for flint.

Kate was having a stare down with the spawn, holding the sword like a baseball bat.

"We have to work on your fighting skills," I informed her.

"Really, Craig? Can you just not right now?" Her yell turned into a yelp as the thing lunged forward. She swung the sword wildly, catching the spawn across its chest and it fell away, clawing at itself as if burned. "What's it doing?"

I honestly didn't know.

The chest of the thing smoked as if burned from the touch of the sword. It was forged in Boshen many, many centuries ago and I thought it was out of regular obsidian steel. But obsidian steel did not react like that.

"Do it again!" I bellowed, still trying to light the torch.

"Seriously—gah!" she yelled.

I watched as the spawn stood to its full height, bearing down on her, but she was a trooper, I had to give her that. She swung that thing as though her life depended on, which it did really.

She managed to catch it on one of its elongated arms, slashing right through it as if the thing didn't have bones. The arm dropped to the ground, and the ooze dispersed. "That's disgusting!"

"Keep at it!" I cursed as the flint refused to catch.

"Let me help." Forrest limped towards me, looking pale and covered in sweat. He took the flint and expertly lit it in seconds. "Now what?"

I removed the bottled potion from my other pocket and let a single drop fall on the flames. They billowed between us, turning bright green and I wasted no time rushing towards the spawn.

It reached for Kate with its only arm, and she was ready to chop that one off next, when I shoved the torch clear into the spawn's body.

Its back arched and it whipped around, trying to catch me with its arm, but I dropped to the ground, leaving the torch embedded in its back. The flames covered in it seconds, filling it from the inside out, so the flames spurted from its jaws, yawning open in a scream that quickly died.

It fell to its knees and then exploded.

Bits of tree bark and black ooze covered us all, and the torch fell to the ground, still burning. I was quick to pick it up and hold it aloft; there was a chance we would need this flame again.

"Everyone alright?" I asked.

Kate wiped crap from her face with a disgusted look, but nodded. "All in one piece, somehow."

"Forrest?"

I turned in time to see his eyes roll back in his head and he collapsed. We ran to his side, and I rested my hand on his forehead. He was clammy to the touch, but he shivered as he laid on the ground.

I didn't know what the spawn did to him, but it didn't look good.

"We have to get it out of him," I muttered, turning him on his side and pulling up his shirt.

Three drag marks ran down his back, all filled with a greyish pus.

"So, it's like a poison?" Kate asked, looking around the forest, but I doubted she would find any of her witch's herbs here to help.

"Yeah, but you're not going to find help here."

"I don't need medicine necessarily," she whispered. "I just need something to get the poison out... and then seal the wounds. That fire of yours, would it work on him since he's a dragon?"

"Huh?"

"I don't know anything about dragons," she muttered as she pressed and prodded around the three deep gashes. "Are they fireproof, or could that burn it out of him?"

"His skin won't burn, but the poison should burn out of him, I hope."

I glanced around, the hair on the back of my neck standing on end. The fight made a commotion, and we hadn't gone unnoticed. We couldn't stay here for long.

I was all for leaving Forrest for being an idiot and not listening to me when he had the chance, but clearly, Kate was not about to leave him behind. No matter how much she seemed to hate him. Well, she probably hated me, too to be fair.

She took the torch from my hand as we rolled Forrest onto his stomach. "Hang on, this is going to suck," she told him.

I held his shoulders down and prayed to whatever gods would listen that he wouldn't shift while we tried to save his life.

Kate held her breath and pressed the torch right into the gash.

Forrest screamed and thrashed, but his dragon remained contained. The poison bubbled and oozed, evaporating in the flames. When the first gash was clear, and the stench of burnt skin filled my nose, she nodded to me and moved onto the second gash.

Forrest screamed briefly, then went completely limp. Good. He didn't need to be awake for this. The third one was the worst and Kate had to touch the flame to it three times before the last drop of poison disappeared.

"There, he'll live, right?" she asked, checking his pulse at his neck.

"We'll have to wait and see." I tore more of my shirt and used it to cover the open wounds the best I could for now.

He would heal now that the poison wasn't in his body, or that was the theory, at least. If it had stayed, he would've turned into one of those plague spawn eventually.

I glanced at her. "Good thinking, by the way."

"Thanks, but I'm sure you would've done the same."

"You have a very high opinion of people you've just met."

We propped his limp body up so I could tie off the makeshift bandage and then we looked around. "We need to find shelter and quickly."

"Are you saying you would've left him to die?"

"I'm saying where I come from, if you want to survive, you learn to make the hard choices. Come on," I said and with her help, got Forrest to his feet, one arm draped over each of our shoulders.

I took the torch back and let Kate carry the sword since it wasn't as heavy for her.

"Where are we headed?"

I wasn't an idiot. I heard the anger in her voice, but she could yell at me all she wanted once we weren't out in the open any longer. Forrest wasn't too heavy between the two of us, and we dragged him through the trees, heading higher up, judging by the increasing steepness of the ground.

I did not want to drag Forrest's dragon ass up a mountain, but thankfully, I spotted a darkened opening near the base.

"Over there," I said, motioning with my head. "We can keep an eye out easily from there."

"You sure nothing's living in it?"

"One way to find out."

Leaving her with Forrest a way back from the cave, I took the torch and quietly crept forward. It was deeper than I anticipated, but that was good.

We could hide farther back, and nothing from the outside passing by would see us. The cave was empty, and I hurried back to get Kate and Forrest.

We propped him the best we could in the back of the cave, lying him on his side so it wouldn't hurt his weight. I gathered up a few sticks from outside, the few that weren't tainted, and built a small fire.

The air had grown colder, and Kate was shivering, holding her arms around herself as I started a fire, blowing on it so it would catch the kindling. Jeans and a t-shirt weren't going to keep her warm enough. I shrugged out of my leather coat and held it out for her.

"No, then you'll be cold," she argued.

"If you took off your bracelet, your dragon would probably keep you warmer," I told her, "but since we're not ready to deal with that yet, take the damned coat."

"And what are you going to do?'

"I'm half-demon. I don't get cold as easily."

She took the coat and quickly slid her arms into the sleeves, sighing as she sank into its warmth from my body. "Thanks."

"Welcome."

We sat in awkward silence with Forrest's heavy breathing the only other sound.

"This sword of yours," she asked, running her fingers over the blade, "you didn't know what it was going to do?"

"Not in the slightest."

"Why do you have it then?"

I stoked the fire gently and wondered how much I should tell her. I didn't know who she was, but to be fair, she had no idea any of this craziness existed until she saved my sorry ass. "I was going to trade it to some sorcerers for a very important artifact."

"And you what, forgot to make the trade?"

"No, the trade was interrupted by demons trying to take me back to my father." I stabbed the stick hard into the cave floor. "Ruddy bastards."

"It's a good thing I guess, since the sword seems to hurt them. Think it could kill one?"

"There's a chance, but if you're going to start walking around wielding a sword, it'd be a good idea if you knew how to use it." I licked my lips and frowned. "We need to find water and food."

Kate lifted her head and sniffed the air.

I watched her, amused by the confused look on her face that turned to excitement as she turned her head. "You said there was nothing else in this cave."

"There isn't."

She jumped to her feet and sniffing the air before her, moved along the back wall. She pressed her hands against the stones, and they shifted. "There's water, fresh water. I can hear it through the stones," she whispered, pressing her ear against them.

I shoved my shoulder against them, and they shifted more. "Ready?"

She nodded, and together we pushed against the stones. They ground together, groaning at being moved, but slowly they gave way and tumbled backward.

Shimmering light from outside reflected on the walls, bouncing off the shallow pool and stream of water running into the cave. It seemed to end at the pool, but it had to lead somewhere.

Kate rushed to the rim and bent down to drink it, but I stopped her. "What?"

"Just hold on." I hurried back to grab the torch, the flame still burning, and returned. "Just in case." I shoved the torch into the pool, but no black ooze appeared. All it did was put the torch out. "Have at it."

She scooped the water in her hands and drank. I did the same and once I had my fill, told her to find a flask in my coat. She unscrewed the top and took a whiff. "What is that?"

"Very strong demon brew. I don't recommend drinking it. Dump it out and fill it with water. Won't hold much, but I'll see if I can fashion a carrier out of something."

She filled the flask and carried it back to Forrest.

I heard her coaxing him to drink at least a little as I wandered the chamber. Moss grew along the wall near where the water flowed in, along with a few mushrooms, but nothing else. No etchings or carvings, nothing that could aid us on our journey back to any realm that wasn't this one.

I took another long drink and returned to the other part of the cave to find Kate hunched over.

"Kate?"

I worried we didn't get all the plague from Forrest, and she was infected, but when I circled around her, I saw the shard of glass in her palm.

Her eyes narrowed on it as her finger traced the pattern.

"Where did you get this?" she asked, in a voice

that was not hers.

"I took it from the sorcerers," I replied quietly. "Do you know what it is?"

Her hand closed over it in a tight fist until blood seeped from her hand. "Stole it from us, took it, and destroyed it! Then the shadow came… the shadow will destroy us all."

I blinked and tried to reach for her bleeding hand, but she yanked it back with a growl.

"Kate, look at me," I said, trying not to show how freaked out she made me. "Give me the shard."

She opened her mouth, baring fangs that had not been there before.

"Kate, give me the shard, right now."

But she wouldn't give it up. She snarled at me, swiping with her free hand and I saw the talons extending from her fingertips. Whatever that bracelet did to contain the dragon, it wasn't working very well anymore.

I backed off, and she turned her back on me.

"Sorry," I whispered, picked up the sword, and whacked her over the head with the hilt.

She grunted and collapsed to the cave floor. The shard slipped from her hand, and I scooped it up to keep it safe with me.

"You can kick my ass when you're normal again."

I stared around the cave at Forrest, still unconscious, and Kate.

How did I always find myself in these shitty situations?

FORREST

My back burned as I tried to move, skin tugging as it tried to heal.

"Be careful moving around," Craig warned, and I opened my eyes to see him coming towards me, holding out a flask. "Water, drink. It'll help."

I took it, not ready to argue with my mouth so parched, I was surprised my tongue was still whole. "Thanks," I gasped, and he nodded as he helped me sit upright. "What happened?"

"Aside from you almost dying because you didn't listen to me? A lot."

I frowned but followed his gaze to see Kate with her hands bound along with her feet, unconscious from the look of it, but close to the fire to keep her warm. "What are you doing?"

"We need to talk."

"Obviously." I tried to reach around to feel the wounds. "You... you both saved my life?"

"You can thank Kate for that, I was going to leave you."

Reluctantly, I held out a hand. "Thank you, I owe you a debt."

"How about you just forget about this bounty on my head? We have bigger problems, you know, the killer plague and all?"

I wanted to deny what I saw, but that... that monster, it was real, and it had come for me. Nearly killed me. How was it no one else believed Craig? If this was already spreading through the demon world, it wouldn't be long before it reached the others, if it wasn't there already.

"Yes, yes I believe you're right."

He laughed sharply. "I'm sorry, could you say that again?"

"Don't push your luck, half-breed," I grunted and stood, stretching my arms. "What happened to her?"

He hesitated then reached into his pocket, and I smelled the item before I saw it. "She held onto this and started to shift, while wearing that bracelet."

I reached for it, but he yanked his hand back.

"Nope, I'm not having you go all crazy either and try to bite my head off."

The scent coming from that piece of glass was old, very old and powerful. "Fine, keep it, but where did you find it?"

"Do you have any idea what it is?"

I shook my head, breathing deeply again. "No, but it smells... peculiar. I can't describe it."

"Do you think you could use it to find more like it?"

I shrugged. "Depends. We're good at finding treasure, but this isn't just treasure. It's so much more." My hand itched to hold it, but I wasn't going to go after him over it. I was too weak to hold my own in a fight right now. "And Kate went into her dragon form when she held it?"

"Partially, it was odd," he said, turning to look at her. "I knocked her out so I could get it out of her hands. She wasn't herself."

"Did she say anything?"

He bobbed his head. "Said they stole it from us, or something like that, then the shadow was going to destroy us all."

"That's comforting." I moved around the fire and checked the bracelet on her wrist.

She growled but remained unconscious. The inlaid runes were ancient, and most were beyond my skill of reading, but whoever created the band knew what they were doing. "This bracelet was not meant to hold her dragon forever."

"Is that what it says?"

"I can only make out a few of the runes, but essentially yes."

We both stared down at her. Who was she and why was she living with a witch? Her story was complicated, I sensed that, but I needed to understand who she was and if she was a threat, or a dragon in need of my help.

It was rare to find shifters who were not part of a clan. Many of our kind lived between worlds. We accepted the modern age of humans and benefitted from many of their technological advances, but never had a dragon in her condition crossed my path.

"How long has she been out?" I asked.

"A few hours," he said with a cringe when I glared at him. "What? I can't take on a dragon by myself, and we're in a cave if you didn't notice."

He was right, but I didn't have to approve of him whacking her over the head. "This shard, where did you get it?"

He told me the story of finding an old text in the demon archives before he was thrown out, one that told of a glass shield that would show the way to defeating the shadow. A glass shield sounded pointless to me, and I said so, and to my surprise, he agreed.

"I didn't think it was real until a sorcerer contacted me saying they had a piece."

"How many are there?"

He flipped over the shard in his hand, lips pressed into a thin line. "They didn't know."

"Well then, that's a great start," I muttered sarcastically.

He tucked the glass shard in his pocket as he scowled at me. "You know, at least I'm trying to find a way to stop our worlds from winding up like this one, completely infested with no hope of saving it."

"But you know nothing of what this shield might do."

"All the text said was the one who was meant to wield it would bring together the pieces and stand against the darkness, forcing it back to oblivion. That's all any of the texts said," he mumbled and sat down hard. "I watched people I grew up with die of this," he whispered bitterly. "Watched as the darkness took them and my father did nothing to save them. So many dead and he just let them die—his people."

"Leaders are forced to make tough decisions—" I started.

Craig shook his head. "No, my father saw the disease, and he banished them to the outer reaches of our world," he snapped. "He turned his back on them when they needed him most."

It was no secret the dragons loathed Raghnall, but I never truly understood why until now. Letting his people die was a sin, one that could not be forgiven. "You tried to stop him I'm guessing?'

"Yes, and then he disowned me, wanted to put me in a cell. So, I ran."

"This shield you speak of, who is the person meant to wield it?"

"That's another question I need an answer to," he admitted. "I know it won't be me."

"But why not? You're the one who's been fighting

against this shadow, you're the one searching for the pieces."

"And I'm a thief, a murderer, and a bastard. I don't deserve to wield such a weapon."

Forrest walked around the cave, his back tingling as it healed. "I'm sure we'll find this person, whoever they are."

"Now you're on board with my plan? You couldn't have decided that before we were sent through a portal and into this world?" he asked, but when I turned to rebuke him, he was grinning.

"Does nothing dampen your spirits?"

"Eh, I'd rather stay on the positive side of life than on the dark side."

Kate shifted, and her eyes opened as Craig, and I cautiously stepped closer.

She tried to move her feet, and when they got stuck, she tried to sit up. "Ah, guys? What's going on?"

"You're not in crazy mode, are you?" Craig asked.

"What? No. Untie me!"

He freed her wrists, and her legs then stepped back quickly.

She frowned at him then looked to me for an answer.

I had none to give. "He said you went dragonish on him."

"I did?"

"You don't remember?" he asked, as his hand reach into his pocket.

"Don't bring it out again, not yet," I ordered. He glowered at my commanding tone but removed his hand. "Kate, you need to be honest with us before we go any further."

"I need to be honest? That's rich," she snapped, scooting closer to the fire. "I'm stuck in this world with a half-demon and a dragon, but the human needs to be honest? About what? I told you, I've lived with Mama Lucy for years, didn't know she was a witch, and no I didn't know I was a dragon."

"But someone did," I insisted. "Your bracelet, who gave it to you?"

She stiffened, and I saw pain pool in her eyes. "None of your business."

"It is if that thing's not going to contain you forever," Craig added.

"What are you talking about?"

"Your bracelet," I informed her and gently reached out for her arm. She let me take it, and I sensed the power coursing through her body, stronger than any dragon I met before, even my father. I ran my fingers over the runes but gained nothing new from staring at them. "It was meant to fall off when you were ready."

"Ready for what?'

"We don't know, and so yet again I ask you, who gave you this bracelet?"

She worried at her bottom lip and whispered so quietly, I almost couldn't hear, "My father."

I glanced to Craig, worried that her own father

would try and keep her true identity a secret. "What was he?"

But she was lost in her own memories as her eyes closed and she hung her head. "Doesn't matter. He's dead. They killed him… just like they killed my mother. Dead, they're all dead," she breathed.

"Maybe this can wait a bit longer," Craig tried.

But I needed to know. "What is your full name, Kate?"

But she shook her head violently and tore herself away from me. "No! Those were the rules, never take the bracelet off and never speak my name. Never!"

I followed her, but Craig grabbed my arm and stopped me. "Back off her, prince," he snapped in warning. "She's already unstable enough, and the last thing I want is for her to go into a form she doesn't know how to control."

I bared my fangs at him, but he was right. "You will have to tell us soon," I commanded. "Our lives may depend on it."

"What are you talking about?' she asked sharply.

"You've been dragged into this mess for a reason, and I have a feeling, it was not merely to fall through a random portal with a half-demon and a dragon." I stepped closer and looked her right in the eye. "You have a destiny, Kate. It's time you start embracing that fact."

"Again!" Forrest yelled, and I cursed. "I said again. Defend yourself!"

"I can't," I snapped, slumping to my knees. "This is not what I had in mind when you said embrace my destiny."

Craig smirked from the log he sat on nearby, and I glared at him.

"You must learn to fight if we are to survive this world. Pick up the sword and defend yourself!" He charged me as he spoke.

I pushed myself up, digging deep to find whatever strength I had left. He wasn't fighting with a sword, and it should've been an easy fight, but he managed to dodge every swing of the blade and smacked me on the back with that damned stick of his again.

I screamed in annoyance and pain and dropped the sword, launching myself at him, fists flying as I had the first time I attacked him.

Craig burst out laughing as Forrest took several hits to the face before he managed to kick me off and I went sailing across the tiny clearing we found not far from the cave.

I landed with a painful thud and spat dirt and grass from my mouth.

"This is not a tavern brawl," Forrest snapped. "You will not be able to take your opponents down with your fists all the time."

"Works for you," I muttered and climbed to my feet. "I need a break."

"You can break when you successfully defend yourself." He picked up the sword and offered it to me, hilt first. "Take it."

I rolled my eyes, but took the sword, growing heavier by the second. I settled back into the defensive stance Forrest showed me and worked at steadying my breathing.

I closed my eyes for a brief moment to try and clear my head, but there were too many chaotic thoughts rushing around.

Forrest took a step forward, I sensed it more than saw it, and spun out of the way of his attack as I opened my eyes.

I was angry, so angry at what happened. Seeing Mama Lucy attacked like that, and the kids scared half to death.

Forrest lunged again, and I ducked under the stick, spinning out of his reach the opposite way.

I was mad at being thrown through a portal, and into a world, I had no idea how to navigate.

I hated Forrest and Craig because I felt a strange connection to them for what they were. For what I supposedly was.

Forrest moved again, and I closed my eyes, finding it easier to listen to his breathing.

I moved as if the air around me pushed me, guided me and for the weirdest moment, I heard a voice I hadn't heard in nearly ten years speaking to me...

Use your feet, feel the path to take.

My dad. It was my dad's voice rushing through my mind.

The world around you is a part of you. Let the air give your movements strength, tell you where your enemy lies. Feel it, Katherine, feel it deep in your bones. Your senses are strong, do not lose focus... just breathe...

Two strong hands covered my own on the hilt as I moved swiftly, gracefully, in my attacks against Forrest. I moved faster and faster, hearing him stumble in the dirt.

I heard Craig's quiet curse as he rose from the log and just when I was ready to destroy my enemy, my arms came to a sudden stop.

I opened my eyes to see Forrest on his back on the ground, the sword tip at his neck.

I blinked a few times then backed off, dropping the sword. "Oh my God, I'm sorry. Are you alright?"

I expected him to be mad, but he grinned as I pulled him to his feet. "How did you do that?"

"I don't... I don't know," I said, not ready to tell them I heard the voice of my dead father in my head, felt him guiding my movements. "I need some water."

Forrest nodded, and he and Craig watched me jog back to the cave. Once inside, I rushed back to the spring and splashed water on my face, hand shaking violently.

What was happening to me? The images I saw in my head, they were real. Sometime long ago, my dad taught me how to fight. Why would he do that?

We will never be safe... they do not understand who we are... enemy, they only see us as the enemy...

"Dad?" I whispered to the cave. He wasn't here, I knew he couldn't be, but his voice was all around me. Whispering. I covered my ears, but the voice continued until I shoved my head under the water, desperate to make it stop.

The rush of cold drowned out all other noise until all I heard was the muffled rushing of the stream pouring into the pool. When I lifted my head back, I shoved my wet hair from my face washed the dirt and grime from my arms and neck.

Everything was fine. I wasn't turning into a monster, and I wasn't going crazy. We were going to find a way out of this world, get back to Mama Lucy, and I could go back to my normal everyday life.

You're an idiot. You can never go back, and you know it.

I begged my inner nagging voice to shut up and returned to the cave to find Forrest and Craig returning, something furry hanging from their hands. "What are those?"

"Think of them as rabbits," Craig said brightly. "If we're moving out in the morning, we need food." He sat down by the cold fire pit and started to remove the fur as Forrest leaned the sword against the wall.

"Right, and we're sure this is our best option?" I asked.

We'd talked about it at length last night and this morning, about how to get back home.

Craig was the only one of us who knew this world. According to what he read, there was a temple at the top of the tallest mountain rumored to have access to a portal in it. He said it made sense since the plague had to have a way to spread from one realm to another. All it needed was a power boost to get us back home. Between the three of us, he didn't think it would be a problem, but I knew what this plan would require of me.

The bracelet might have to come off. I wasn't sure if I was ready for that, but if it got us home, then I'd do whatever it took.

"We can't keep waiting around for more plague to find us, or worse," Craig said.

"Or worse? What could be worse?" I asked alarmed.

His knife paused in its carving up of the beast, and the only sound was Forrest building the fire back up and lighting it with a puff of fiery breath. "Worse would be coming face to face with the thing that started the plague in the first place."

"Wait, it's here?" I suddenly felt like our cave was no longer safe. "Why didn't you say that?"

"I was trying not to freak you out anymore. Look, it hasn't come for us yet, so it might not even know we're here."

"And where do you think this shadow being is?" Forrest asked tightly.

Craig kept his gaze focused on his task as he replied, "The temple."

"What?" Forrest yelled the same time I did.

"And we're just going to waltz in there and use the portal?" I asked in disbelief. "You've got to be kidding me. We're going to die, we're all going to die. This is great."

"That's no way to think," Craig commented, spitting the rabbit-like animals and setting them against the fire. "It might not be there, and if it is, chances are it's sleeping."

"The shadow sleeps?"

Craig nodded and sat back, watching the flames lick at the meat. "According to the archives, the shadow spreads and feeds for a time, but then it hibernates. It's why it's taken it so long to move to the demon world and why it's spreading slow. The shadow is still weak, but soon, it'll have its strength back, and the demon world will be exactly like this one. Dying with no way to stop it."

The headache I thought was gone rushed back full throttle. This was too much for any one person to deal with. I couldn't do it, but what else was I going to do? I wanted to get back to Mama Lucy, needed answers, and that temple was the only way to get to her.

We sat in silence as the food cooked, and once it was ready, Craig passed one to me and the other to Forrest, letting us take some before he ate.

For a guy who claimed he was a bastard, he was keen on keeping us alive. I tried not to read too much into it. He needed us as much as we needed him. None of us would be getting anywhere close to home on our own.

The meat had a weird salty taste to it, but I ate my share and went to wash it down with some water. Knowing how horrible tomorrow could be, I found a soft spot on the cave floor, close to the fire, and tried to get some rest.

I wished for restful sleep, but the moment I closed my eyes, all I saw was that night again. Hearing the people breaking into our house as Dad told me to run and not come back. Hearing the strange language that the people coming for us spoke, me sprinting through the trees as I prayed I'd survive, that my dad would survive. The bright flash filled my vision, and I jerked awake.

"Kate?" Craig asked worriedly. "You alright?"

"Yeah, yeah just a bad dream," I whispered and shut my eyes even harder.

This time when I relived the nightmare of that night, I picked up on something I never noticed before: the roars I heard at the exact time of the blinding white light sounded familiar. As in, something I'd heard recently.

They sounded exactly as Forrest's roars had when he shifted earlier.

The men that came for us that night, they weren't demons of some unknown origin.

They were dragons.

15

CRAIG

"How sure are you this thing is at the temple?" Forrest asked me a while later when we were both certain Kate was asleep.

Earlier, when she'd woken, I saw some horrible revelation in her eyes. Whatever she dreamt of frightened her beyond just a normal nightmare. I wanted to ask her more, but she went right back to sleep and was snoring quietly now.

"Fifty-fifty," I replied honestly. "Most of what I've found on this thing was from centuries ago."

"This shadow has been around that long? Why do we not know of it?"

I rested back against the cave wall, crossing my feet at the ankles and lacing my fingers behind my head. "No idea. You'd think when something this horrible threatens our world, we'd all rise up to stop it instead of trying to erase it and act like it never happened."

"Do you think whatever's driving this did something to our memories?"

"I'd say there's a good chance, but unless we can find someone who was alive that long ago and ask, we'll never know for sure."

The firelight flickered off the sword resting against the wall. Teaching Kate to fight was necessary, and I expected her to be horrible at it. She never held a weapon before in her life until that spawn attacked us. But watching her move as she went after Forrest, there was a strange grace to it, as if she'd been doing it for years.

"Muscle memory," I whispered.

"Pardon?"

"Sorry, it's just... the way Kate fought today, I've seen that style before."

"It was strange, how easily she slipped into those stances," he agreed quietly. "She said she's never fought before."

"Not that she could remember."

It had been impressive to watch the gliding style of swordplay, how she used the air to push her attacks and she did it all with her eyes closed. It shouldn't have been possible unless she'd done it before.

Forrest was right. We needed to understand who her father was if we were to figure out who she really was. The only other time I'd seen fighting like that was in the inter-realm festivals where fighters would show off their skills in the arena, non-killing of course. The festival was meant to bring peace between the races.

Before I was forced to leave my home, I remembered watching a dragon knight from an ancient line. He was one of the last of his kin, and he fought with such a fluid grace, it left the crowd speechless and his opponent in awe. No other dragon clan displayed such skill, and I never thought I'd see it again.

Until today when Kate suddenly did it as if it was nothing.

"Do you know of a clan that died out?" I asked Forrest. "A clan of warriors?"

"We're all warriors," he said dryly, "and sadly dragon clans all come to an end when it's their time."

"This one would've been recently."

Forrest's face wrinkled in thought. "The only clan that has disappeared in the last one hundred years is one we do not speak of. They were traitors, all of them."

"What did they do?"

"They attempted to assassinate the royal family, my family. They were mad, all of them, claimed we were all going to burn in some horrible fiery end if they didn't spill the blood of my family to save us." He rested his head back with a scowl set on his face. "It's said their ravings didn't stop until their heads were removed from their bodies."

That didn't make sense to me. We all had our

crazies, but for an entire clan to rise up and say the end was near? "And no one thought to try and question them once they were secured?"

"My father did, but nothing they said made sense. He couldn't trust them enough to let them loose, so he had them executed, and the rest were banished, told never to return. They'd already run for it; we never expected to see them again." He picked up a pebble from the ground and tossed it absently between his hands, seeing a scene from many years ago from the strange look in his eyes. "Shame really, they were the most magnificent warriors. Their wingspan was legendary as were their acts of bravery on the battlefield. I grew up on stories of their accomplishments."

My stomach sank as I looked to Kate and back to Forrest. "Did someone curse them?"

"After they were killed, their lands became poisoned," Forrest said. "Nothing has grown there since and it's said nothing ever will. The curse that it was rumored fell on them was transferred to their lands, and it's forbidden for any to travel there for fear they'll be cursed, too."

I almost didn't want him to go on, but my curiosity got the better of me. "Has anyone gone there ever, just to see?"

"No, dragons are superstitious, you know that," he said bitterly.

"And yet something tells me you know of someone who went there anyway."

He caught the pebble in his fist and crushed it, so dust fell to the ground beside him. "A friend, on a dare. He went and when he returned… he was not himself. He was placed in a cell and has never been released for fear of what he will do." He met my gaze as he whispered, "He tried to burn me alive. Said I was poisoned."

"What was the name of the clan, Forrest?"

"No, we were told never to speak it. It's bad luck."

"Because our luck could be so much worse right now," I said, holding up my hands. "What was the name?"

"Why does it matter?"

"I don't know, but the more information I can get my hands on, the better."

He still looked skeptical, and I was ready to wring his neck to get him to spit it out, but then he sucked in a deep breath and whispered, "Darrah. The clan's name was Darrah. Before my family ruled, they were in charge of our clan, but things happen as they so often do, and power changed hands." He scooted down the wall, crossed his arms, and closed his eyes. "Now if you don't mind, I'm going to sleep."

I nodded and turned to watch Kate.

Her breathing was even as she slept on.

Is that who she was?

A Darrah, one of these cursed dragons?

If she was, she couldn't let Forrest know. He was too honorable for his own good. He'd kill her on the spot, and I needed her to help me stop this plague.

I thought my life was difficult before; now, now it was becoming damned near impossible to not wind up dead.

16

KATE

We set out early, or I guessed it was early. There was no night, or morning in this world. No way to tell time and it bothered me. I wanted to know how many hours I'd been away from Mama Lucy and if she was alright. If the kids were unhurt.

I itched to get back home and figure out if Forrest was right and I did have a role to play in whatever the hell was going on.

Or I was crazy, this was all inside my head, and I was currently living out this fantasy in an asylum. Both were possibilities as far as I was concerned.

I carried the sword since I refused to remove my bangle yet. Craig had relit his torch with the potion before we left the cave, and Forrest brought up the rear of our trio, traipsing as quietly as we could through this dying world.

I had no idea how far we walked. My mind was

too cluttered with denial of who I was and what I remembered my father teaching me so many years ago. Why would I need to know how to fight?

But those men who came to the cottage... they weren't men at all. Carefully, I shot a glance over my shoulder, but Forrest was too busy watching our surroundings to see me watching him.

Dragons.

Dragons had killed my dad and probably my mom, too.

"There it is," Craig uttered, and I tripped over my feet trying to stop, running right into the back of him.

Forrest reached out to steady me with a worried look, and I flinched away from him.

Craig's brow arched at it, but he didn't say anything about it. "It's more rundown than I thought and completely out in the open."

I turned to see where he pointed, and my blood ran cold as a strangled noise escaped my lips.

"Kate?"

My eyes darted to Craig, but I still couldn't get the words out. The temple, or what was left of it, had clearly been part of a much larger structure, like a castle perhaps. The same castle and surrounding landscape I saw in a vision.

"We shouldn't be here," I managed to whisper.

"We have to, we need to get home," Craig insisted, but I shook my head harder and backed away again.

"No... no, we can't be here. Do you have any idea what this place is?"

I blinked, and all I saw were the dead bodies scattered across the ground, bloodied and broken. The screaming intensified and when I blinked again, dragons flew in the skies, fire raining from their mouths against a shadow that only grew more and more despite their fierce attack. The rain that fell wasn't rain. Oh no.

It was blood. I felt it hit my skin and rubbed against my arms, desperate to wash it off.

"How do you know what this place is?" Forrest asked sternly.

The beast he said lived within me reared its head, and I snarled at him, a fiercer growl than before, vibrating through my chest. His lips thinned, but he took a half-step back warily.

"I've been here before," I snapped.

Craig half-smiled until he realized I wasn't kidding. "You can't have been."

"I was, or I saw it," I said and rubbed harder at my arms, but the vision of blood was gone, as were the bodies and the aerial attack that had been so vivid only moments before. "Dead, so many dead and the shadow. It was here."

"You mean it is here," Craig said, but I knew what I'd seen. "You're not making any sense. How do you know all of this?"

I didn't want to tell them, but maybe it would convince them we couldn't go there. We had to find another way to get home, any way that did not involve being here where so many violent ends to life occurred.

"I saw a battle here," I whispered, as if afraid somehow I'd get sucked right back into that moment. "I touched a dagger in that witch's shop, and I saw this place, but it wasn't destroyed, at least not completely."

"You had a vision?" Forrest asked confused.

"No, maybe? I don't know, alright! All I know is I saw this place and the shadow, plague whatever… I'm pretty sure it destroyed it." I chanced a glance back towards the ruins and inwardly sighed in relief when no more dead bodies appeared. "There were people running and screaming as they died and an army of dragons in the sky trying to fight it, but we… we couldn't."

"We?" Craig asked with a worried look to Forrest. "What do you mean, we?"

I tilted my head as I whispered, "I was in the body of one of the dragons."

"Wow," Craig said, shaking his head. "This just hit a whole new level of insane."

"You saw the final battle that ended this place? How is that possible?"

I ignored Forrest and only focused on Craig. "I don't know. But I know that shadow was here, and it killed everyone. I didn't have to see the end of the fight to feel that." I rubbed my arms to try and chase away the sudden chill, but it lingered.

Forrest reached out as if to drape an arm around me for warmth and I pulled away.

"Don't touch me."

"What's wrong with you?" he snapped. "I am your kin, and yet you show anger and fear towards me yet friendship towards the demon!"

"I have my reasons."

"Like what?" he challenged, smoke trailing from his nose.

"It doesn't matter. We're going to get back home and then you both are going to disappear from my life."

Craig cringed. "Not sure it's going to be that easy."

"And why the hell not?" I wanted to stomp my foot but resisted the urge. I wasn't five, but decking them both for the hell of it, that sounded like fun. Sadly, I resisted that urge, too.

"That shard I have? You've got a strange connection to it," he told me, "and the vision you told us about... I don't think your part in this is close to being over. Whatever's coming for all of us, it won't just stop at the demon world. It'll come after the humans, too."

I ran my hands through my hair, messing it up as I paced around in a tight circle. How did I get dragged into this mess? "Fine, fine, I'll work with you," I finally said and pointed to Craig. Then I pointed at Forrest. "But not you."

Forrest's hands curled into fists at his sides, and his eyes glimmered in warning. "Explain."

"No," I shot back and crossed my arms. "I don't owe you anything."

"As far as you know. You might be part of my clan, and if that is the case then you are defying a direct command from your prince! That is treason."

"Just drop it," I seethed, but he glowered right back, closing the distance between us. "Back off."

"No, I want to know right now why you hate your own kind so much."

"Guys, maybe this can wait for another time," Craig said in an attempt to break us apart, but Forrest growled at him fiercely.

"Don't you dare go after him." I shifted, so I blocked Craig from view.

"Stop protecting the demon! Tell me what you're hiding! Tell me who you are!"

"Why? So, you can kill me too?" I yelled at the end of my rope. The words slipped out, and I couldn't take them back now.

Forrest's glare went from enraged to confused in a few seconds.

He stepped back. "I don't understand. I would not harm another dragon."

"Tell that to the dragons who killed my parents."

Forrest looked as if I slapped him.

Craig's jaw dropped. "Kate, are you sure?"

I nodded firmly at Craig and waited for Forrest to explain himself now. "Tell me why. Tell me why you would destroy a family, tear it apart. What did we ever do to you?"

"It's not possible," he whispered. "You must be mistaken. Someone else was responsible," he tried, but I was already shaking my head. "Kate, please, we would not attack a family for no reason. It's not done."

"Ten years ago," I told him fiercely, "people found me and my dad. I was told to run, and I did, hiding in the woods until morning and what I saw that night... what I heard... there was nothing left of my home. No dad, no body. No house. Nothing. It was obliterated in a bright white light accompanied by roars. Dragon roars." I poked him in the chest hard enough to make him back up. "You tell me why you would kill my father. Why?"

Forrest's mouth worked as he struggled to find words, but before he could say anything, Craig cursed and grabbed us both, dragging us to the ground.

"We don't have time for this," he whispered as the chill I thought was from my memories increased, making it so cold my teeth chattered. "It's getting closer, and we're running out of time."

"Kate, please," Forrest said in my ear. "I swear to you we did not kill your father, but I will help you find out who did. I won't rest until they are avenged."

I wanted to believe him, but a voice in my head told me I couldn't trust him. I couldn't trust any of our own kind. I grimaced at that sentence. I was clumping myself in with the dragon crowd now like it was the most natural thing in the world to do. I needed to get home before this got any weirder.

"I promise I won't try to kill you, yet," I replied. "Happy?"

"No, but it'll do, for now."

We looked to Craig who merely blinked and mumbled in some guttural tongue under his breath. "Great, this just keeps getting better and better."

"What's the plan?" I asked, hoping to get us moving again. I didn't like sitting here but getting to the ruins meant crossing through an open field where we'd be completely exposed. If the shadow was nearby, the chances of it seeing us were high. I thought about the beast I saw in my vision, rising up like a swarming mass over the land and a shiver shot down my back. There was no way we could fight against it, not if an entire army of dragons failed at bringing it down.

They were weakened, Dad's voice whispered through my mind. *Weakened and betrayed.*

I scowled at the ground, needing the voice to stop. Now was not the time to take a trip straight into Crazyville.

"Get to the temple without being seen. Once we're inside, I doubt we'll have long to find the portal and get it up and running before it comes for us."

I rolled my shoulders as the beast inside me shifted again, lifting its head as if to say now was the time. The bangle glowed brightly on my wrist, but I quickly covered it with my other hand.

I noticed Craig glance at it, but he turned back to the ruins.

"When I say, we make a break for it," he told us. "Stay low and keep moving, no matter what."

Forrest and I nodded as the three of us pushed up and made ready to sprint for our lives.

My heart beat out an unsteady, painful rhythm in my chest as I attempted to keep my breathing regular and failed.

Craig peered around the clearing, and I heard him count out to three. He took off, and I followed, Forrest right on my heels.

I worried I wouldn't be able to keep up with them, but the knowledge of potential death awaiting me if I stopped was a good motivator.

I pumped my arms, sucking in painfully cold breaths of air. The ruins grew closer, but the plain stretched on much larger than it first appeared.

Gentle hills rolled beneath our feet, and I tripped, skidding into the rocks we'd been crunching over.

But when I glanced down, it wasn't a rock I came face to face with.

It was a skull. I scrambled away from it in a panic only to see more. The field wasn't filled with rocks.

It was covered with bones. Piles and piles of bones.

17

FORREST

I expected Kate to scream at the sight of the undead surrounding us, but she bit it back, biting her lip hard enough to make it bleed.

Craig and I dragged her back to her feet.

"Don't look at them," Craig ordered, and taking her hand, pushed onwards.

I glared at their linked hands. It should be me she drifted towards. We were of the same kin, but she didn't trust me, and now I knew why.

She believed her family was dead at the hands of dragons. I didn't understand how it would be possible. I would've heard of an order going out to destroy a family. Had they been traitors? Victims of another family rising to power within a clan? We did our best to act in non-violent manners, but no race was immune to such atrocities.

One way or another, I would seek out the truth

and get her to understand and trust me, as she should.

The ruins towered over us and we reached their shadow, but the ground dipped, and we had to wade through more bones, piles, and piles of them. Kate whispered a stream of curses under her breath, but Craig helped keep her on her feet. We had to keep moving. The temperature, which was already frigid, dropped again and the air puffed out in little clouds before our faces.

"Nearly there," Craig said, urging us on faster.

The hill towards the ruins was steep, but we pushed through and finally, pressed our backs against the scorched black stones. Nothing came out of the trees to kill us, and no shadow-plague beast appeared. For the moment, we were safe. I glanced at the stones surrounding me and carefully ran my fingers over the black soot marks on them.

"Dragon fire," I murmured. "My kin were here."

"Told you."

I pursed my lips at her cold tone, but didn't respond. If dragons fought and died here, I would know of it, so why did I not? Once we returned to the dragon world, I would confront my father about this place and try to find some much-needed answers.

Kate and Craig could assume we were going back to the human world, but despite how horribly wrong this mission had gone, orders were orders. They were coming back with me, even if I had to drag them unconscious through the portal to do it.

Kate was a dragon, and she belonged with the dragons. We would sort out the mess of her family once we were home.

And Craig, well, as much as I respected him for not killing me, if we tried to hide him from Raghnall, we could potentially start a war.

"We have to sneak around to an entrance and get inside," Craig whispered. "Stay as quiet as you can."

He led the way, moving around the ruins until we came to an opening in the wall. Stones and debris filled it, but we climbed over. Rocks scattered at our movements, and we froze as the sound echoed loudly across the clearing. We held a collective breath and waited.

But still, nothing came. Perhaps the half-demon was wrong, and there was nothing here.

We made it fully into the ruins. The ceiling overhead had been arched before it was destroyed and only parts of the structure remained standing. None of it looked safe, and I waited for our cautious steps to bring it down on our heads. Though being killed by stones was better than being turned into one of those feral plague beasts. My back throbbed in remembrance of the first attack and I did not want to feel that pain again.

"Where's the portal?" Kate asked as we spun around in a circle.

The temple was empty, aside from the few walls

still standing, and a large stone altar set in the center of the space. On it were stone holders for candles long since gone. Whereas dust covered every other surface, the altar was clean as if someone took the time each day to wipe it down.

"It's here," Craig whispered, closing his eyes and holding out one of his hands. "I sense it."

I watched as he moved around the altar, his hand moving as if it ebbed and flowed with some invisible current.

Curious, I stepped closer and was taken aback by how strong the power was here. It took my breath away, and I had to steady myself before I could move again.

"So, yes portal?" Kate asked.

"Oh yeah," Craig replied and approached the altar, resting the torch beside it. "We have to activate it."

"And how do we do that?"

"Magic." He waved for her to join us at the altar and reluctantly she did so, standing at one of the shorter ends while Craig and I stood opposite each other at the longer sides. "Place your hands on the stone."

I did it, my hands moving as if drawn by a magnet.

Craig followed me.

Kate hesitated. "The bangle. What if it doesn't let me?'

"Then you have to remove it," I told her. "It's time you embrace who you are anyway."

She glared. "Maybe I don't want to be part of a race that murders families."

"Kate, we don't have time for this," Craig growled surprising us both. "You can kill him after we get out of here."

He looked around paranoid, and just as I was about to ask him what was wrong, I felt the strange shift in the air, too.

"It's quiet," I breathed, but it nearly came out as a yell.

The ambient sounds around us were gone as if we'd been pulled into a void.

"Kate, please," Craig said. "Now or never."

She scowled, but set the sword aside and placed her hands flat on the altar. "Now what?"

"Focus," he instructed. "Focus on pulling the power from deep within you and pushing it into the altar."

She blinked a few times at him like he was crazy. "Seriously? I've never done that before. I don't even know what's in me, and you just want me to pull on this power?"

"You are a dragon," he stated firmly. "You are strong, we've all seen it. There is something inside of you, and it's time you face it. If you want us to get home, you have to let yourself feel, let yourself understand what you are."

She looked like she wanted to argue again, but scrunched her eyes shut tight and breathed heavily out her nose. "Focus... focus..." she repeated a few times.

I did the same as did Craig. I hadn't been able to access my power, except for shifting since arriving, and feared now we wouldn't be strong enough to open the portal.

Then a jolt shot through the stone, and I looked at Craig.

He shrugged; it wasn't from him.

Together, we turned to see Kate's hands glowing a vibrant blue, her palms melding into the stone as the light crept up her arms.

Intricate designs that had not been clear before covered her bare arms, traced up her neck and finally her face, ancient runes that matched the same styling as the ones on her bracelet.

"Uh, Kate?" Craig asked gently.

"Hmm?" she asked. "Is it working?"

"Maybe you should open your eyes and look," I suggested.

She opened one eye then the other and jumped. "Holy crap. What is this?"

"That is some very strong magic," Craig answered. "Very old magic."

I couldn't believe what I was seeing. No dragon alive had power running through their veins like what she displayed here. No one.

"Who are you?" I whispered, confused and in awe at the same time.

The bangle on her wrist was glowing, too, so

bright I couldn't stand to look at it. Maybe this would work after all.

The altar vibrated and hummed with the amount of power pulsing through it, and a gust of warm air blew around us.

Not far away, a black hole appeared and steadily grew larger and larger.

"Is that it?" Kate asked excitedly.

"Yeah. Keep holding on," Craig instructed. "Once it's holding steady, we'll let go together and dive in."

"How will it know where to take us?" she asked.

"We guide it with our thoughts," he replied. "All you have to do is think of Mama Lucy's house, and that's where we'll go."

No. No, that was not where we were going to go.

My plan had been to steer the portal back to the dragon world, but I had not realized how strong Kate's magic would be.

Her thoughts would override mine, and we would go where she wanted.

Guess I was going to have to knock her out anyway; it was for her own good.

As the gust increased in speed, the portal grew larger, a crack between two worlds. Once it was ten feet in diameter, it held steady, pulsing with magic as it waited for us to use it.

Craig nodded, and we began to pull our hands back when a sharp screech erupted from the altar.

I winced, covering my ears as something warm trickled from them.

Kate cried out in pain and Craig growled as we fell away from the altar.

I expected the portal to shut, but it remained open, powered by the strength of Kate.

The ground rumbled, stones shaking before starting to collapse around us.

"We have to go!" Craig yelled, and waved us towards the portal.

I rushed to join them, but the altar exploded as a dark mass shot upwards into the sky. We went flying, slamming hard into the walls and stones. I slid to the ground, grunting as every part of my body screamed in pain.

I heard Craig yell, but it was muffled, like someone shoved cotton in my ears.

Kate was lying not too far from me, but she wasn't moving. Her eyes were shut, and her breathing looked labored. She was hurt bad; the attack knocked her out.

I crawled towards her, ready to carry her and yell for Craig to follow as we dove for the portal, but the shadow slammed back down on the remains of the altar.

A bone-like cracking came from the swirling darkness, and a figure took shape within its depths.

From first glance, I would've said it was a demon, but it was far too large, too broad to be one. When it turned, I caught the silhouette, and my stomach dropped.

It had the head of a dragon. I stared, transfixed by

the sight as it towered over us, red eyes smoldering with fire. Talons stretched at least a foot from its hands, and as it took a step towards us, the ground shaking, the swirling shadows remained with it.

"You," it hissed in a voice that made me grit my teeth to hear it grate against my mind. "You should not have come here."

"Don't worry, we're leaving," Craig told it, pulling himself to his feet. He held the sword in his hands, thrown with us when the altar exploded. "Let us pass, and we won't give you any trouble."

"But trouble you have already given me." It lifted its massive head, sniffing the air. "And what a gift you have brought to me. So much power. So much strength! You will not leave, oh no, not now. Now, you will be a sacrifice to my master."

"Master?" Craig repeated, and I heard a tremor of fear in his voice.

His eyes found mine, and we thought the same thing at the same time. If this thing wasn't the plagued shadow causing the darkness to spread, then what the hell was?

"You will not touch her!" Craig hoisted the sword as high as he could, but it was a struggle.

His arms trembled, and I knew he wouldn't be able to stand against this spawn for long.

For a brief second, I almost grabbed Kate and lunged for the portal, but he saved my life, and I owed him a debt.

Whether I liked it or not. If I saved him now,

when I turned him over to his father, I could do it with a clear conscious.

I had no weapon except my dragon form, and I rolled my shoulders as it awoke within me.

The beast laughed at us both, a dark, evil sound that tore at my soul. "You think you can stop me?" It reached out a hand and without touching me, lifted me off my feet by my throat. It choked me.

I gasped, kicking my leg trying to free myself, but it held fast.

Craig charged it with a yell, but he was in the air a moment later, about to join me in my fate.

"You will die, and then the power will be mine!"

The pressure on my neck tightened and black dots formed in my vision.

I couldn't shift, couldn't breathe.

This was how I was going to die, in some Burnt World, beside my enemy.

There was no hope.

18

KATE

Something was wrong.

Get up, Katherine.

Dad. That was Dad's voice, wasn't it? But that wasn't right. He was dead. I shouldn't be able to hear him, but that was him.

I tried to open my eyes, but they refused to budge. The air was heavy around me, almost like trying to breathe in water. I wanted to move, see what was happening, but my body refused.

It's time. You must get up, Katherine. You must fight!

"Die now!"

My eyes shot open, and I gasped for air, eyes wild as my mind tried to play catch up.

A dark shadowy figure, another plagued spawn, stood in the center of the temple, and gripped in its talons were Forrest and Craig.

They tried to fight back, but they were losing, and

both looked like they were on their last bit of strength to hold on.

They were going to die. Was I really going to sit here and watch them die?

The hell I was. I came too far in this crazy life of mine to give up now.

I made it to all fours, searching for anything I could use as a weapon.

The sword! It was a few feet away.

If I moved, I was sure the creature would see me, but I didn't have a choice. It was move and be seen, or watch as that thing tore them to shreds.

I moved as carefully as I could, but when my arm was before my face, all thoughts of moving stopped.

The glowing marks that appeared on my body when I'd touched the altar were back, and they were pulsing in time with my racing heartbeat.

The bangle warmed against my skin, and I heard Dad's whisper again that it was time.

"No, not yet." I wasn't ready to see myself turn into a dragon yet.

What if I couldn't control it? What if I accidentally wound up killing Craig and Forrest instead of helping them?

The sword was close. Ignoring the voice in my head, I crawled towards it.

"You will not fight me," the plagued spawn snarled and took a large step towards me, shaking the foundations of the ruins. "You will be part of us!"

"Kate... run!" Craig rasped, pointing towards the portal that was still open.

"No! I'm not leaving you!" I snatched up the sword, sucked in a deep breath to ready myself for the attack... but nothing happened.

My feet were stuck to the stones as if someone glued them down.

I went to swing my body around, but it refused to respond to my commands. "Let me go!"

Its evil cackle struck me like a slap to the face, and I winced in pain... and then I growled.

My foot slid forward an inch, but it was still an inch.

"You are a fool," the demon snarled. "You will not beat me!"

"That's what you think." I moved forward another inch and another.

My arms trembled, fighting against whatever power held me back. I managed to bring my arms forward, and the shadows swirled faster around the demon, some lashing out to strike me. I took the pain. I needed to break free of its hold so I could save my friends.

Well, one friend. Forrest was still up in the air.

My feet moved again and again and with a final push, my arms glowing so brightly I was blinded, I lunged forward with the sword, slashing at the demon figure.

It shrieked as the sword struck something solid

and Craig and Forrest were released. They coughed and hacked, backing away from the shadows reaching back out, trying to snatch them up again.

"The portal! Get to the portal!" I yelled as I continued the attack.

The shadows moved as one, and suddenly, I was trapped within them. The sword was yanked from my hands, and I heard it clatter somewhere far away.

"Kate!" Craig yelled, but as he made a grab for my hand, the shadow shot out like a whip, slamming him back into the wall.

"Get out of here!" I twisted and turned as the shadows raced around me, blocking out my view of the light, of the portal and my way home. I thrashed wildly in its grip, but darkness was all I saw. It was becoming a part of me, and I couldn't break through.

"Give in," a voice growled, different from the demon I could no longer see. "Give in and join me, Darrah, Vindicar. It is your destiny."

Fight, Katherine! You must fight!

"I can't," I cried back, sinking to my knees as the shadows pressed down around me.

Yes, you can! You are a Darrah, the last of our kind. Your destiny is only beginning, my daughter. The time to fight is now, so fight!

I curled up in a ball, waiting for the end to come, but my dad's words rang through my ears, and I knew what I had to do.

Yelling with the effort of pushing back, I reached for my wrist with the bracelet.

With one hard tug, it broke, and the shattered pieces fell powerless to the ground.

19

CRAIG

My heart was in my throat. I couldn't see Kate.

The shadows swallowed her up completely, and nothing Forrest or I did let us pass them.

I growled in fury, feeling my demon side ready to burst through and attack mindlessly, but that would get us nowhere. I reined it back in.

"She's dead," I whispered to myself in numb disbelief. "She's dead."

Forrest didn't argue, and it made me feel worse. I dragged her into this mess, and she was dead because of me.

The portal was on the other side of the ruins. We had to get past the shadows to reach it, but I couldn't just leave. Not without knowing for sure if we could save her.

We needed to distract the plagued demon. Make

him leave her be, but I couldn't make out his silhouette anymore. The shadows were too dense.

Forrest yelped, and I spun around to see a tendril of shadow wrapped around his legs, dragging him towards the altar.

"Craig!"

I jumped to try and grab his arm, but another tendril lashed out, pinning my arms to my side as I collapsed to the ground.

They dragged us roughly across the stones. This was it. I was going to die and with the only two people who believed me about the plague spreading. About this world existing. It was over, everything was over...

I blinked and squinted at the ball of shadows. I had to have imagined it. I shook my head, fighting to break free and saw it again.

The tiniest blip of blue light amongst the darkness.

"Forrest!"

"What?" he snarled, his dragon still attempting to break free even as the dark magic stopped him.

I motioned to the shadowy mass, needing to know if I finally lost it, or if there was really a blue pulsing light now. "I see it! Kate!"

We yelled her name, screaming at the top of our lungs.

She was alive! She had to be alive!

The pulsing increased as the brightness grew until it burst through more of the shadow. The plagued spawn snarled in rage, and its shape slowly came back into focus, but the tendrils held us fast.

I couldn't see Kate, but she was alive. That was her magic, and when I blinked again, I couldn't believe what I saw.

A roar that ripped across the open plain around the ruins and tore down the rest of the standing structures exploded from deep within the shadowy mass.

A being of pure light rose and spun around, stretching wings that stretched far larger than Forrest's had when we first arrived and he fought the plague spawn.

The massive dragon flexed those wings, sending a gust of wind to knock us all back to the ground as it lifted itself higher in the sky.

"Kate," I whispered in awe at her form. My spirits lifted at the same time my heart sank. I'd only seen one other dragon who looked like that, and it had been the warrior at the festival.

A Darrah. She was a Darrah, and I wasn't the only one who realized it.

Blue rivulets of power rippled over her body as she lowered herself back to the ground.

Swinging her head wide, she bashed through walls of stone, opening her jaws wide as fire brewed in her chest.

It shot from her mouth and struck the spawn and its surrounding shadows, but the flames weren't red and orange.

Oh, no.

These were blue and almost electric in appearance. They crackled like lightning through the air, and the hair on my arms stood on end.

The spawn pushed back against the attack, but she easily dodged the shadows, swung her body around, and her tail slammed into him.

When she swung back around, she faced me and sniffed the air. She bared her fangs at me, and I stood perfectly still, waiting to see if she would try to kill me, too. But then she bobbed her large head, and those green eyes glimmered.

She knew exactly who I was, and I thanked the gods for that. Forrest crept beside me, and she growled fiercely at him, but didn't attack.

"I will destroy you!" the plagued spawn shrieked and flew back at Kate, sending them tumbling out into the field in a tangled mass of shadows and dragon limbs.

All I could see was a ball of dragon fury and shadow, but Forrest and I would be idiots to try and break them up.

We needed her to hurry and get back through the portal. It wouldn't stay open for long and as I glanced over my shoulder, saw it was already shrinking.

"Forrest! Get the sword!"

"Why do you still need it?"

"Just grab it!"

"What are you going to do?"

I tilted my head back and forth as I readied to

sprint out of the ruins. "Something I'm probably going to regret." I took off, running as fast as I could to catch up to Kate and the spawn. "Kate!"

I waved my arms over my head, but she was in too much of a fury to notice me. The shadow tried to surround her again, but she swiped at it with her tail and when that failed to throw it off, threw her head back, unleashing a wild spray of blue fire, dousing the field.

I cursed, dodging it as I ran closer.

"Kate! Damn it, Kate! We don't have time for this!"

I looked around for something to get her attention and picked up a heftily sized rock.

"Hey!" I yelled and chucked the rock at her head.

She whipped around snarling and snapped her jaws a foot from my face.

I stared her down and waited for her to realize that our time in this world was over and we needed to leave, now.

"No! My master, he will have you!" The spawn was stalking towards us again, and I staggered backward, tripping over the bones in the field.

I was about to take off running, but Kate scooped me up in one of her clawed feet and her wings spread out wide behind her.

We lifted off the ground, crossing the field in seconds.

Forrest was right beside the portal, and she reached out another foot to grab him, spun in a tight three-sixty, and we sailed through the portal.

Then there was falling and more falling and then nothing.

❧

"Ow," I winced, when I lifted my head. "Where the hell are we?"

"Lie still before you hurt yourself any further."

I knew that voice. "Mama Lucy?" I managed to pry open my eyelids and saw her brow furrowed with worry as she hovered over me. "We're back?"

"Yes, thank the goddess," she murmured. "What happened?"

"A lot." I pushed myself up, and she let me this time, bustling away from my spot on the floor to the couch I'd laid on not too long ago. "How long were we gone?"

"Barely a day," Forrest answered for her.

I shifted my gaze and saw him sitting on the floor, leaning against the far wall, face pinched in anger. His hands were limp on his lap, and his head lolled to one side, too.

When I started to smile, he snarled at me.

I gave him a weird look. "Are you having issues, friend?"

"I am not your friend," he seethed. "This witch paralyzed me."

"Temporarily," she amended sharply. "Serves you right, coming back through that portal and trying to tell me you're taking my girl away from me. Terribly rude, even if you are a damned prince."

Kate.

Wildly, I searched the living room and breathed a sigh of relief to find her on the couch. She was breathing and looked unharmed, except her eyes were closed and the marks on her body were still visible. They weren't glowing as strong as they'd been in the ruins, but they were there, all the same, pulsing in time with her breathing.

"How is she?" I asked as I made my way stiffly to her side and took her hand. I expected Lucy to shove me away, but she only stared down at Kate and shook her head.

"I don't know yet. That portal opened in the living room, and the three of you burst through it. You were all unconscious. He woke up first," she said, nodding to Forrest. "Barely offered me a word of explanation of what happened before he demanded I stand aside and let him leave with you both, so perhaps you'd be so kind as to tell me."

"Are you going to paralyze me if you don't like what I tell you?" I asked.

Lucy frowned. "Depends."

"Okay then," I said, wondering where to start. "Well, let's just say Kate definitely knows she's a dragon now. A very unique dragon."

"She's a traitor," Forrest chimed in, but Lucy snapped her fingers and his voice cut off.

He kept trying to talk, but no sound came out and

eventually he gave up, slouching against the wall, and contented himself with glaring furiously at us both.

Lucy pulled her shawl tighter around her shoulders. "I will not have him tell me what Kate is."

"But is she a Darrah?" I asked. "She didn't outright tell us."

"I wish I could say, but she's never told me about her past. But that bracelet, I knew it was old, very old, and I knew one day she would come face to face with who she truly is."

I gave Kate's hand a gentle squeeze, willing her to open her eyes. "She's doing just that. Forrest told me about the Darrahs. Told me how they killed them all off." I focused intently on Kate's face. "All but one."

"I'll die before I let him drag her away," Lucy stated.

"He won't be taking her anywhere."

I felt Forrest's glare intensify, but didn't spare him a look. All that mattered now was Kate waking up and all of us working together to combat what we saw in the Burnt World.

Lucy said she would make some tea and then I could tell her all about what happened while we waited for Kate to come back to us.

❧ 20 ❧

KATE

"Kate, open your eyes. Kate."

I didn't want to. I was comfortable, finally comfortable. All I wanted to do was stay here and not have to deal with whatever the world wanted to throw at me next.

"Kate."

I wasn't sure who grabbed my shoulder, but I finally opened my eyes, and my jaw dropped.

"Dad?"

He stood before me in his plaid shirt, dirty jeans from working outside, and grey short hair. He smiled warmly and threw his arms open.

I leapt into them, and he hugged me, kissing the top of my head.

"Wait, if you're here... am I dead?" I asked, pulling back suddenly.

His laugh was warm, and I hadn't realized how much I missed the sound of it. It'd been rare when I would hear it and should've treasured it more since our time together was so short.

"No, you're not dead."

"Then how are you here? What is this place?"

Everywhere I looked I saw nothing, but a gentle, blue and white light. I couldn't even tell what we stood on, but didn't care. My dad was here.

"I've always been with you, but you never needed me until now."

I frowned, unsure of what he meant until he held up my wrist, my wrist without a bracelet. "Oh no! Where is it?"

"You removed it, just as you were meant to."

I rubbed the spot where I'd worn it for so many years, trying to remember what happened.

There'd been yelling, lots of yelling.

Craig and Forrest.

They'd been in trouble, and the plagued shadow attacked us as we tried to escape.

I stared in amazement from my hands to my dad's face, filled with pride.

"I'm a dragon."

He nodded. "Yes, one of a very powerful, old bloodline."

"But… why? How?" I shook my head as the past events hit me all over again. "Why didn't you ever tell me?"

"You weren't ready to know, and it was too dangerous. It still is." His smile fell away, and he held my shoulders. "Kate, you must listen to me. There isn't much time, but you are in grave danger now that you've shifted. You've revealed yourself, and they will hunt you."

"You mean dragons like Forrest?"

"Not just dragons," he corrected, and my gut twisted. "I'm afraid you will never be safe again."

I puffed out my cheeks and wished I could close my eyes go back to sleep, pretend none of this happened. "Why? What happened to our family?"

"Our history is a long and difficult one. I do not have time to explain it all now. You must find it out on your own and learn from it. It's the only way to stop it for good this time."

"You mean the plague?"

"Yes. We thought we contained it before, but we were wrong. There is only one sure way to end this. The shield of the Vindicar."

I wrinkled my face. "I don't know what that is... but the spawn... it called me that."

His face tightened in fear. "It recognized your power. How you must wield it. We had it for a very long time, the shield, but when our family was betrayed, it was stolen and shattered into pieces. You must find them, Kate. Find them and bring them back together."

"And do what?" I asked frantically. "I can't do this!"

"Yes, you can. This is what you were born to do, Kate, and if you can't, then the world is lost."

I clung to his arm, wanting him to come back

with me, but he was fading from sight right before my eyes. "Dad, please."

He cupped my face in his hands and kissed my forehead. "I have faith in you, my daughter. Remember all I've taught you, and you will be fine."

He hugged me again, and I clung to him as tight as I could, willing him to stay with me, but I felt his presence slipping away.

Tears slipped down my cheeks to lose him again.

And then he was gone, and I was falling backward through the bright lights.

ॐ

"IT'S THAT STRONG ALREADY? HOW CAN THAT BE?"

I knew that voice.

Mama Lucy's voice.

I was back home, safe and sound, in Mama Lucy's house on the comfy couch in the living room. Maybe it was all a dream after all, and I was going to open my eyes and see Mama Lucy with the kids.

But when I did open my eyes, I looked right up into the eyes of Craig, the half-demon. "Damn."

"Kate?" he asked confused.

"Sorry, I was hoping all of this had been a really bad dream," I mumbled and tried to sit up, but stopped when my neck screamed in pain and my head throbbed. "Ow! Why does everything hurt?"

"Probably because you shifted into a dragon for

the first time and went after the plagued spawn," he offered. "Saved our asses, though."

"I did?"

He nodded and smiled warmly. "Yeah, you did."

With his help, I sat up, and Mama Lucy was there to hug me.

She was crying, wetting my shoulder, and I patted her back.

I told myself whenever we were safely back home, I'd let myself fall apart, but now, after speaking to my dad and fighting off that… that demon spawn, falling apart was the last thing on my mind.

A strength I never knew I had in me burst into life and I realized there wasn't time to sit around and complain about the turn my life took.

I was a Darrah, and though I might not know exactly what it meant, I knew it was important. People were relying on me, the world actually. I had to be strong now. Had to be fierce enough to save them all.

"Mama Lucy, you're smothering me," I mumbled after a few minutes of letting her hug me so tight.

"Sorry, sorry!" she mumbled and leaned back, smoothing my hair from my face. "Craig was telling me about what happened. Are you sure you're alright? I didn't see any injuries, but everything happened so fast."

"Yeah, guess it did." I glanced at Craig, but he looked unharmed for the most part. I looked around the living room and paused when I spied Forrest.

"What's wrong with Forrest?" I asked, seeing him propped up against the wall, not saying a word.

"He wants to take you back to the dragon world because you are, in his words, a traitor." Mama Lucy lifted her chin and glared at him fiercely. "I should turn him into a toad."

"Can you do that? I mean, with all the other magic you can apparently do?"

She sighed and patted my cheek. "I'm sorry you had to find out that way, hon. I was going to tell you at some point, if you really wanted to know." She glanced once more at Forrest. "And no, I can't turn him into a toad, at least not permanently."

That was too bad. I knew I couldn't trust him. Dragons killed my family, and as soon as Forrest learned who I was, he wanted to take me out to. Dad was right, it appeared. Thinking of Dad reminded me of what he said, and there was no time to waste.

"Craig, do you have that glass shard still?"

His eyes widened in panic, and he dug through the pockets of his leather coat laid out across the back of the couch. He breathed a sigh of relief as he pulled it out.

I reached for it, but he pulled back.

"You sure about this? Last time you went a little crazy."

"I'm sure."

He waited another moment, holding my gaze, before he rested it in the palm of my hand. This time when I closed my fingers around it, I was ready for the power radiating off it. This was a part of me, this power, and there were many more pieces out there we needed to find.

I opened my eyes and smiled at Craig. "I'm good, but I think I need your help."

"My help? For what?"

I held up the glass shard, so it caught the light. "This is a part of a shield, one that once belonged to my family," I explained. "Or at least that's what my dad said."

"And when did he tell you this?"

"A few moments ago," I replied quietly.

Lucy and Craig nodded slowly. "You saw him?" she asked.

"I did, and he told me this is part of the Shield of the Vindicar." I let the glass rest flat in my palm. "And according to him, I'm meant to wield it somehow against this thing that's coming so this time we can stop it for good."

"And did your dad happen to tell you where the other pieces are?"

"Nope, and I have no idea where to look for the other ones."

Craig tapped his fingers on the couch, but then his lips curled into a grin, and he glanced over his shoulder at Forrest. "Maybe you don't, but I do," he mused. "The dragon archives. They'll be filled with information we could use, clues to track these pieces down. You are after all a dragon and if I'm not mistaken, a Darrah."

I still wasn't sure what exactly that meant, but Craig seemed to.

"Care to share?"

"It means you are royalty, just as Forrest is. And," he added, holding his finger up, "if I also recall my history lesson correctly, courtesy of Forrest himself, the Darrah clan was the rightful rulers over the Chimalus clan until his family rebelled and took over."

"Is that right?"

"Yes, yes, it is, so therefore you do not have to listen to him," Craig told me. "And it also means that you have every right to return to the lands of your ancestors."

"No," Mama Lucy argued. "It's too dangerous. You'd be going right where he wants you."

I swung my legs around, so my feet were on the floor, and with Craig supporting me, managed to stand upright. "If we don't do something about this plague, it'll spread from the Burnt World, my old world I think, to the demon world even faster and eventually, it'll come here. We have to stop it, Mama Lucy." I might know everything there was to know about this new world around me, or demons and dragons, or witches, but I would have to figure it out as I went.

What I did know was that plague spawn was not the true enemy. The voice in my head had been, and it was much more powerful than the spawn we faced. If we weren't ready when it came, we'd all die.

Slowly, my legs shaky from shifting into a dragon and back again so quickly, I approached Forrest. This time when I stared into his eyes, my dragon shifted in response to another being so close. But it wasn't happy. Smoke trailed from my nose, and a growl reverberated deep in my chest.

"I think it's time you and I have a real honest chat, Prince Forrest," I said, crouching down before him. "What do you say and remember, it's treason to disobey your princess."

His eyes narrowed in rage, but that was just fine with me.

The time had come for me to learn all about my history and I was going to start with learning how Forrest and his kin betrayed mine to their deaths.

KEEP READING FOR AN EXCERPT FROM THE NEXT IN THE *Dragon Reign* Series.

SHARDS EXCERPT

Kate wants answers. She wants to know about the family she's never known. She and Craig are convinced they have to return to the cursed lands to find the answers.

She finds herself with more questions that she thought she'd have as she's torn between half-demon Craig and son of the dragon shifter clan Forrest.

Craig's got feelings for Kate, but he also has secrets of his own. He didn't count on her seeing his secrets in the flesh.
Forrest's torn between his own feelings for Kate and his allegiance to the clan.

Kate—she's just torn.

1

KATE

"If you two can't stop growling at each other for five seconds, I'm finding duct tape."

Two sets of annoyed eyes turned to stare at me, but I raised my brow and waited to see what they would do.

My head throbbed, my body was sore, and I was anxious as hell.

I rolled my shoulders again, feeling the beast moving freely within me now. On some level it was cool, knowing a dragon lived within me.

And on the other hand, it freaked me out. How was I supposed to function with this thing inside me all the time? Each time my anger flared, I sensed it wanting to break through and take control, but if I destroyed Mama Lucy's house, pretty sure she'd kick my ass for it.

Harry, the big shaggy dog, was still hanging

around and sat on his haunches close by, resting his head comfortingly on my leg. I'd been absently scratching his ears for the past few hours. It helped keep me calm, somewhat.

"If one of us was being cooperative, there'd be no need for growling," Craig murmured.

A deep rumble came from Forrest's chest, and we both eyed him. It cut off suddenly, and he lifted his hands. The manacles and chains holding him captive rattled, echoing his disdain. "Are these necessary? I am a prince and you, Kate, are in no danger from me."

"Ah, but you see that means Craig is, and right now, I'm on his side."

"You should not be."

"So, you're saying I should blindly follow a guy I just met—"

"Dragon," he corrected.

I ground my teeth, digging my nails into my thigh. "Dragon I just met, one who by the way has already said any bearing my name are traitors and deserve to die, and what? Go back with you to meet your daddy who by all rights will be pissed by the fact that one, I'm a Darrah, and two that I've chained his son up." I shook my head, my hair wild around my face as I tried to restrain it in a braid, mostly to keep my hands from reaching out and strangling Forrest. "No thanks, I'll pass."

Harry harrumphed as if in agreement and trotted away to stare out the front window.

Forrest's hands fell to his lap as he looked on, torn between annoyance and defeat. "I blame you."

Craig pointed at himself with a mocking surprised look on his face. "Me? And why do you blame me? You're the one that said plain as day what you do to Darrahs."

"I would, of course, plead her case to my father. She didn't know who she was."

"Plead her case? Wow, aren't you a hero," Craig snapped, and scooted closer to me, protectively almost.

During our time in the Burnt World, I had to say I found reasons to find both of them attractive, but I told myself my emotions ran high in the heat of the moment. Feeling anything besides aggravation at both of them should've been impossible in that moment.

But when Craig stepped closer again, as if ready to bodily put himself between me and Forrest, a little thrill shot through me and my dragon practically purred in delight.

"Alright, can we please get back to figuring out who my family is, or was?" I checked the door to the living room, but Mama Lucy hadn't come back yet. She'd taken the kids to a neighbor's until we decided our next move.

"I don't know what you want from me." Forrest rested his head back against the wall and closed his eyes. "I have told you everything I was told. I can't make myself remember something I don't know."

"There has to be more." I tossed my braid over my shoulder and held my head, willing the throbbing to stop at least for a few minutes so I could think. "How long ago was the last sighting of my family?"

Forrest shrugged. "Fifty years give or take."

"Fifty years?" That couldn't be my dad then. He wasn't that old when he died.

"Yes, but dragons and demons, all… non-humans, we live longer," he pointed out.

I lifted my head at his words and frowned between the two of them. "So, you two are old?"

Craig barked a growling laugh. "No, I'm twenty, soon to be twenty-one which I hear can be quite exciting in the human world."

"Yeah, means you can drink."

Craig's brows drew together giving him a brooding, cute look that made me want to reach out and smooth them back out. "You can't drink yet? That's awful."

"Not legally. What about you?" I asked Forrest, giving his foot a kick with mine when he didn't seem inclined to answer.

"Same."

"And that means my dad could've been that last dragon then, right?"

"It's possible. Do you have a picture of him?" Craig asked, but I was already shaking my head.

"Everything we owned was in the house the night it was destroyed." I couldn't help it, I glared at Forrest.

His eyes narrowed, but he learned from my last outburst and didn't try to deny it was other dragons who attacked us.

"His name was Maddock," I whispered. "Maddock Darrah."

Forrest's Adam's apple bobbed, and he suddenly seemed very interested in the floorboards.

"What?" I snapped.

"Huh? I didn't say anything."

"You didn't have to." Craig pushed off the couch and towered over him. "You know that name, I can see it in your eyes."

He sniffed in answer and refused to look up.

Craig took a threatening step forward, but I caught his hand. "No, if he wants to be an ass then let him. We don't have time for this." I expected Craig to ignore me and grab Forrest by the throat and give him a good shake, but after a moment he resumed his seat. "If Forrest won't confirm it then I need your help."

"You saved my life. Pretty sure I owe you."

"You need her," Forrest snarled, his rage boiling over as smoke trailed from his nose. "That's the only reason you're still here."

"I'm still here," Craig seethed between clenched teeth, "because I'm working to stop that plague from spreading. The one you said didn't believe existed until it attacked you and nearly killed us all. Kate here is the key to stopping it so yes, I need her."

My head gave another fierce throb as the weight

of his words struck me like I was fighting that plagued beast again, and I cringed. "All that matters now is stopping that thing from taking over another world and to do that we have to work together." I rubbed at my wrist, needing to find another bracelet soon so I could have something to fiddle with again. "And if anyone gets to have a freak-out, pissed off moment, it's me!"

I jumped up and paced around the living room, rubbing my temples in a frantic attempt to get the pain to leave me alone.

Harry gave me a sympathetic whine but remained at the window. I'd asked Mama Lucy about him before she left with the kids, but she hadn't figured out whose dog he was yet. Or if he was a dog at all. She'd mumbled something about a familiar then left it that. I didn't care really. I liked Harry and Harry was a pretty good watch dog. He'd keep Mama Lucy safe.

"What did your dad look like?" Craig asked.

I shut my eyes tight as my feet paused. "He was tall, really tall and broad at the shoulders, but he was graceful for a man." Memories floated through my mind, more of what I'd forgotten. How he helped me learn to use a sword. "He was the one that taught me how to use a sword. His hair was black like mine, but his eyes… his eyes were amber."

Craig cursed quietly under his breath. "I did see him."

"What, when?" I asked desperately praying it was recent and he was alive.

"Years ago, at the games. I'm sorry. I was maybe seven? Snuck out so I could watch the fighting and there was a Darrah dragon there."

He said he was twenty and I was going to be eighteen soon. "Four years before he was killed," I whispered. "And that was the last time he was seen?"

"As far as I recall," Craig told me. "He just disappeared."

Forrest adjusted his position, suddenly looking uncomfortable.

"Tell me what you know," I pleaded. "Please, Forrest, this is my family we're talking about. I deserve to know the truth."

Forrest chewed his bottom lip so hard, I thought he would bleed. "You're going to hate me more than you already do."

"I don't hate you," I corrected. "I don't exactly trust you not to act rashly."

The beast within me lifted her head and growled quietly, but Forrest opened his mouth, and the words sounded forced out of his throat. "I was there, at the games Craig was and I saw the same fighter. We all did." He took a deep breath and closed his eyes. "Everyone assumed the Darrahs were gone, those that weren't wiped out fled and we did not hunt them down. As long as they gave us no trouble... but then a dragon fighter showed up to the games, and the moment he started fighting, everyone knew exactly what he was. Who he was."

"Why would he do that?" I asked softly. "Why show his face?"

"No one knew. Afterwards..." He licked his lips and looked like he wasn't ready to keep going, but he wasn't going to stop, not now.

"Tell me," I demanded, voice thick with emotion. I sensed what was coming, but I had to hear it.

"I overheard my father ordering our men to track Maddock Darrah down and bring him in. After what you told me, it's safe to assume your father was not going to come willingly."

My gut twisted, and I felt sick as I hurried to back away. Growling sounded in the room, and I realized it was me. My vision blurred, and the beast was ready to break free and scorch this murderous traitor until he was nothing, but bone.

The rational side of my mind reminded me my fire wouldn't burn him, but the dragon in me said it was still worth a try.

Craig called my name, but he seemed so far away.

I shook my head, but the growling intensified. I wanted to be free, I wanted to soar over the clouds.

I wanted to burn the town to the ground, so they could feel my pain.

The doors slid open to the living room, the banging drawing my attention.

Mama Lucy was there, and she rushed towards

me. Her lips moved, but I heard nothing she said. Her fingertips touched my forehead, and I was floating in blissful darkness, the dragon curling back up in a tight ball, watchful, but at peace.

For now.

2

CRAIG

I laid Kate on the couch for Mama Lucy. I tucked a loose strand of her braid behind her ear as she relaxed in sleep.

"What did you do?"

I straightened to see Lucy scowling at me and Forrest. "Don't look at me."

Forrest rolled his eyes and huffed. "I merely told her the truth, which is what she asked for. This is not my fault."

"Eh, seems like it might be a little bit your fault." I held up two fingers an inch or so apart for emphasis. "I mean it was your family that killed her family, and then your father that sent the orders that killed her parents."

Lucy's scowl deepened as she crossed her arms. "You're lucky those chains are all you're bound in." She walked around the room and peered out the window, Harry obediently following at her heels.

Guess he found his new home and it wasn't with me.

Mama Lucy whirled around. "Do you know why your father went after him?"

Forrest shook his head. "I only overheard the orders, but never the reason. I found it strange Maddock would've shown his face at all honestly. It had been years since the fallout."

Kate stirred on the couch, and all three of us held our breath. Her eyes blinked open, and she glanced around. "How did I get on the couch?" She sat up slowly and rubbed her forehead, swinging her legs over the side.

"You have to learn to control your emotions," Forrest informed her.

I laughed in disbelief. "Do you have a death wish?" I asked.

Kate mumbled for him to shut the hell up at the same time.

"All I did was tell her the truth."

"Yeah well, maybe no more talking about my family right now." She held her stomach and looked ready to be sick, but after a few deep breaths seemed fine. "What else do you know about this plague thing?"

"Only the bit I could learn before I was booted out of Boshen," I admitted.

"Well, let's start with that," she insisted, and propped herself up on the couch better to listen. "You said this Burnt World was taken over by it?"

"Or created for the plague to be sent there. There's very little information on it anywhere, an interesting fact," I added as I plopped down in an armchair, "that world didn't exist until a thousand years ago. Before then, no Burnt World was recorded, and the only mention of it was during the trials of the Darrahs who tried to kill the royal family."

"What did they say?"

I leaned back in my chair and let my gaze linger on Kate's. "They claimed after the breach was broken, they had no way to stop the plague, so they sent it to another world, one they created. It was meant to hold the darkness forever, but clearly, something went wrong. I'm guessing if the shield was taken from them, then whatever power they did use to seal it is failing, has been for some time." I shrugged my shoulders. "Makes sense since their lands are said to be cursed. It was probably the plague that drove them to madness. What caused them to fight the dragons they spent so many centuries trying to protect."

"Does not matter what drove them," Forrest grunted darkly. "They tried to murder my family in their sleep."

"I know, but I don't think they did it on their own volition. I think the plague was controlling them."

Kate's face paled, and she swallowed hard. "What is this plague thing?" she asked, diverting the subject.

"No one really knows for sure. It appeared one day, out of a crack in the world, or so the story goes.

It swarmed forth, devouring everything in its path. No one knew what drove it, or where it came from, but there was only one way to seal it away."

"The shield of the Vindicar," Kate breathed. "My dad, when I saw him, he told me we were betrayed. The shield was stolen and destroyed."

My mind raced with possibilities, recalling every detail I could remember on the plague and the Darrah's involvement with it. "It's why they had to send it through a portal. They didn't have their weapon to trap it again."

Kate reached into her pocket and pulled out the shard. "But this time I will."

The shard caught the sunlight sending a prism of red and orange light against the floor and ceiling.

"If we want answers, we need to go back there," I told her earnestly. "We need to return to the Darrah lands and see if there's anything left behind for us."

"I need to know where I come from," Kate agreed, but Lucy was already shaking her head. "Mama Lucy, you can't expect me to stay out of this. Not after everything's that happened."

"That's exactly why you shouldn't go, not there."

"I have to," Kate argued gently. "If I'm the last of this line, of the only dragons able to stop this plague from spreading, I can't sit back and do nothing. Craig said it's already spread to Boshen. What happens if it gets further? If it gets here?" She tucked the glass away and took Mama Lucy's hands. "What about the kids?"

She squeezed Kate's hands. "There's nothing I can say to stop you, is there?"

"I wish there was," she admitted with a bitter laugh. "This is not exactly how I thought my life would go, you know? Figuring out who my family really is. I was hoping for something boring."

Patting Kate's cheek, Lucy said, "I knew from the day I first met you, you were special. Saw it in your eyes, that promise of a great destiny."

"A Darrah." Kate shook her head, and her glance drifted to mine for a brief moment.

A rush of heat stirred in my chest and I rubbed it, unsure of what I felt, but then Kate looked away as Lucy pulled her to her feet.

"If you're going, then you will need supplies. Come with me to the greenhouse. Craig, you two can get cleaned up in the bathroom upstairs," Lucy told us. "And don't you dare take those manacles off him," she warned.

I smirked. "Didn't plan on it."

Kate and Lucy walked through the house, Harry following behind, and I heard the back door open and close.

Forrest was already on his feet when I turned around, and I gave a mock bow and a flourish of my hand, letting him walk ahead of me to the stairs.

"The second we step foot in dragon territory, my father will know." His steps were heavy on the stairs, and the chain rattled. "He will come for me."

"Not if we're careful."

"You don't think the demons will be there searching for you, too? Where do you think your cousin went to after he could not find you here? He won't stop hunting you. None of them will."

I ground my teeth and imagined grabbing him by the neck and throwing him over my shoulder to thud down the stairs. He might even break a few bones, if I was lucky. "Let me worry about my family troubles."

"As you wish."

"And if we get caught that means Kate is caught as well. Do you truly want your father to know she's a Darrah?"

Forrest's shoulders stiffened as we hit the hall and moved down looking for the bathroom. "As I said, I will plead her case, and once we explain what we have seen, I have no doubt my father will see reason and let her live."

"For how long?" I grunted. "I doubt he'll let her keep breathing after she helps return this plague to its cage, if he lets her live that long. For all you know, his men might have orders to kill Darrahs on sight."

"He would not do that."

"No? Then explain to me how her father and mother wound up dead," I snapped.

I glanced to the right and grabbed his shoulder to stop him.

He shrugged me off, whipping around with a growl, but I jabbed a finger into the bathroom then flipped on the light.

"Get cleaned up. I'll be right out here."

He held up his wrists, but I shook my head.

"Don't understand how I'm to properly tend to myself if my hands are bound."

"I managed." I gave him a wide grin, and he sulked into the bathroom, slamming the door shut in my face. "Touchy."

The chains would hold Forrest without a problem, so I pushed away from the door and wandered down the hall. It wasn't hard to sniff out Kate's room.

Her cherry vanilla scent from some lotion or another stuck with me, and I pushed open a door in the middle of the hall. Her room was small, but cozy looking. There was a hanging hammock in the corner; I could imagine her sitting and reading there. The bed was a mess, and there were clothes scattered around the floor and tossed carelessly over the bed. I peeked towards the stairs, but there was no sign of her or Lucy yet, so I stepped further in.

Shelves of books hung over a tiny writing desk with a laptop and stack of textbooks. A sketchbook sat open beside them. Gently I turned it so I could see the images better. Most were of a garden, and a greenhouse. A few were of kids, probably the others that lived here.

When I reached the back of the sketchbook, my fingers stilled to see images of a half-destroyed castle, ruins, and dark destruction left behind by an unseen tragedy.

I flipped to another page, and another and my chest tightened with apprehension when I came to the final few sketches. Images of Boshen stared back at me.

Images of it burning and shrouded in darkness.

The floor creaked out in the hall, and I turned around to find Lucy watching me closely.

"Going to give me a lecture on snooping?" I asked, unwilling to leave the sketches alone.

"It's not my room, but if Kate finds you in here, she might deck you. Or set you on fire." Her lips twitched in a soft smile. "What were you studying so intently?"

I hesitated to show her if Kate hadn't yet, but she needed to know. "These." I held up the sketches to her and Lucy let out a strangled noise of surprise and fear. "Exactly what I was thinking. How would she know what my world looks like if she's never been there?"

"I don't know, but these images, these look as if they haven't happened yet."

"That's what worries me," I sighed. "You think she glimpsed the future somehow?"

"Anything is possible. The Darrahs are a strong family given a task of great importance. There may have been a buried ability to predict when this plague would strike."

"Then Boshen doesn't have much time." I tore out the sketch and folded it up to ask her about later.

Lucy arched a brow at me but said nothing.

"I came up to fetch you both some clean clothes," she said and headed off down the hall.

I waited in the hall as she disappeared in a room at the end then returned a few minutes later with two shirts and two pairs of cargo pants.

"Did you kill the previous owners of these?" I teased, and she tossed them at me with a mischievous grin.

"You'll never know. Now then, I'm running into town to gather supplies with Harry. And to see if I can't replicate the potion you used against the plague, but it will take time, so I doubt I'll have any for you today. Kate is in the greenhouse. I suggest the two of you give her some peace and quiet for a few moments at least. I would prefer to return to a house that's still standing."

She turned to go, but I stopped her as I called her name.

"After we went through the portal here, what happened? What of the others? My cousin?"

"Those who enter a witch's house against her permission always get what's coming to them," she said quietly. "Your cousin will be feeling the beating for a few days at least."

"And the dragons?"

"They ran off once their prince, along with their target, was gone."

I shifted uneasily on my feet. "I'm sorry, truly I am, for whatever harm I caused."

Lucy spun around and bobbed her head. "I appreciate that, I do, but something tells me you were meant to find Kate that day. Otherwise, she never would've started on this journey and that horrible plague, it would keep spreading." Her bright eyes glimmered as she held my gaze. "Fate is funny sometimes, acting in ways you don't expect. All I ask is you do your best to keep her safe."

I scuffed the toe of my boot across the floor. "I don't have the best track record for staying out of trouble, as I'm sure you've noticed."

"You care for her."

Not a question, so I didn't answer.

"You'll keep her safe because you are more than just the bastard son of a demon king," she said firmly.

I was compelled to meet her eyes again. They shone with power, and I had no doubt she'd been able to hold her own against my cousin long enough to chase him off.

"You are meant for great things, Craig, do not let anyone tell you differently."

Swallowing hard, I fiddled with the clothes in my hands and felt a surge of knowing flow through my being. What it meant, I had no idea. "I will do my best to keep her safe, I swear it to you."

"Good." Her voice was thick with worry, but she said nothing else, and left me alone.

I stood in the same spot for a long while before getting my feet to move again.

Whatever happened once we reached the dragon territories, I would not be the one to let Kate down.

3

I hoped being in the greenhouse would calm my quickly fraying, nerves, but as Mama Lucy and I worked at gathering the herbs we would need for our journey, all my thoughts turned to what we would face once we left the safety of her home.

My gut was in full rebellion, and I sipped at the soothing tea Mama Lucy brewed for me before she left. We needed salves and a few enchantments, things to aid us on our journey.

A journey to the cursed lands of my family.

I drained the tea and waited impatiently for it to take effect, but after a few minutes it seemed futile, and I gave up. I'd have to face my future at some point.

As I cleaned up the tea and the cut-up herbs, the tattoos on my arms gave a pulse of blue light.

I stopped what I was doing to watch, but it didn't happen again, though the faint outline of the marks remained. Gently, I traced my fingers over the patterns on my right forearm, feeling the power in my body.

The beast shifted and moved as if sensing its time to break free and spread its wings was close.

"Not here," I whispered to it, pleading for it to wait. "Mama Lucy would kill me if I destroyed the greenhouse and garden."

The beast huffed in annoyance, but I felt it settle back down—alert, but calm.

Once the herbs were in my leather satchel, I left the greenhouse and ducked inside. I heard the water running upstairs, and assumed the guys were still cleaning up and changing. Mama Lucy always kept spare clothes left behind by the previous kids in her care, just in case.

I set the leather satchel on the dining room table and headed upstairs to find a fresh change of clothes of my own, my boots, and anything else I could think of that might be useful.

Which wasn't much. I'd never planned on going on some portal jumping adventure.

Ever.

I opened my bedroom door and froze when it was halfway open.

My jaw went slack, and all I could do was stare at the shirtless half-demon in my room. Either he hadn't heard me open the door, or he didn't care that I was getting a full view of his muscular back and broad shoulders.

I nibbled my bottom lip and studied every inch of that bare skin I could see.

Craig was already attractive in my opinion, but now he was even more so. Tattoos ran down the right side, intricate runes that looked similar to the ones on my arms. They were beautiful and dangerous.

But it was when he shifted, and the light changed on his back that I noticed the crisscrossing of scars along his back. They ran from his shoulder blade down to the top of his cargo pants.

The skin was mangled towards the center of his back, and I covered my mouth so as not to make a sound. The pain he must've gone through to get those had to be immense.

Another long-jagged scar ran horizontally, starting near the first set of scars and disappeared around his left side.

"Consequences of a demon learning to use magic."

His growling voice startled me, and then he turned. There was a smile on his lips, but it didn't meet his eyes. His chest was as sculpted as his back, and he held the clean shirt in his fist, not yet pulling it over his head.

The scar that started on his back ran around to his navel, as well as the tattoos that covered part of his chest.

"See something you like?"

I shook my head, face burning hot, and quickly

turned away. "Sorry, I uh, I didn't expect you to be in my room."

"Closest to the bathroom to keep an ear out for Forrest," he explained, still not putting his shirt on. "I don't mind you staring at them. The scars."

I nodded but didn't move from the doorway or look up.

His boots thudded across the floor and appeared in my vision.

"Kate, really, it's fine." With two fingers under my chin, he gently lifted my head, so our eyes locked.

The first time we met, I was amazed at how intense his gaze was, but now I saw so much emotion roiling around in there, lost in a swirling storm of pain, hate, and something else I wasn't sure I understood.

My breath caught, seeing how close we stood together. I felt the heat from his body hit mine, and my eyes darted to his lips.

His smirk told me he caught the movement and I cleared my throat, taking a large step away before I did something stupid.

Like, kiss the crap out of him.

"You weren't supposed to learn magic?" I said, trying to distract myself.

"No. It's seen as cheating."

"But you did it anyway?" I swallowed hard, and mentally yelled at him to put his shirt on, but he seemed extremely comfortable walking around without it.

"I had to do something to stay alive."

"And when they found out, they what, whipped you?"

He arched a brow, and I felt worse than I had a few minutes before.

"That's horrible. I'm so sorry." Unsure why I did it, my hand reached out and traced the length of the long pale scar at his side. Goosebumps broke out on his skin, and I heard him suck in a deep breath, but he didn't pull away.

"And this one?"

"That was courtesy of my cousin, Reginald. Don't worry, I paid him back in kind before I left."

My hand stayed on its path, around to his back and up the mangled scars. From there, my fingertips glided over the tattoos.

The runes on my arms pulsed with power as if in recognition of the markings.

His body shifted, and he pressed his back into my hand.

In that moment, I wished the rest of the world would go away. Facing down a plague and saving the world was not as appealing as staying here in this spot with Craig. When I made it around his shoulder and to his chest again, his free hand caught mine, holding it flat over his heart where the tattoos stretched across. His pulse was quick, but strong, matching the rhythm of my own.

We had a connection. It was warm and inviting, like curling up on the couch for a cozy day by a fire.

Even the dragon within me lifted her head and seemed to growl in approval.

I was comfortable around him, and I'd never been like that around any guy, not that I ever dated anyone.

Ever.

"Kate." He growled my name, and though his voice was rough, it moved like a light feather touch over me.

He leaned in, bending lower as I lifted my head and stood on my toes. His lips brushed mine sweetly, and I kissed him back, lingering until reality crashed back into me and I pulled away.

"Sorry, I uh… I'm not sure what got into me." I roughly cleared my throat and ran my hands through my hair. "I should let you finish getting dressed and all."

He smiled. "I'll go to a different room so you can have your space."

I managed a nod, not trusting myself to say anything else.

His shirt in hand, he walked out, but not before throwing me a look over his shoulder. One filled with promise that whatever we started here was far from over.

I closed the door behind him and hurried to my closet. I pulled out a pair of dark khaki pants, my brown hiking boots that laced, a t-shirt and a light green and brown flannel to go over it.

I had no idea what the weather would be like in

the dragon world and decided I'd rather be over-prepared than not. I set out a few extra shirts and pairs of thick socks to take with me. I hoped we wouldn't be gone for more than a day, but there was no telling what we'd find.

Once I was changed, and my boots were laced up, I pulled my hair back in a tight, long braid that hung down my back to keep it out of the way. I made sure to grab the shard of the shield, and found an old velvet pouch that used to hold a necklace, and tucked the shard in it before shoving it deep into the knapsack.

Smoothing my hands over my head as I racked my brain for anything else I might forget, I studied my reflection, my green eyes that reminded me so much of my dad's.

"I hope this is right," I whispered to my reflection, but I was really talking to him.

I longed for a way to talk to him again, but Mama Lucy said if he reached out to me once, he might do so again, but I couldn't go looking for him. That could open a whole other can of problems we weren't ready to deal with.

Glancing around my room, my gaze fell on my sketchbook. It was moved. I reached out and moved it back, wondering what else Craig had looked at while he was in my room. Thinking of him and our brief kiss made my lips tingle.

I touched them with my fingertips, and smiled. If only this was a normal situation between a guy and a girl, and not a dragon and a half-demon. Giving myself a shake, I crammed my spare clothes in my knapsack and glanced around my room one more time. I wasn't sure why, but I felt like I wasn't going to see it for a while.

My bag slung over my shoulder, I stepped out of my room at the same time Forrest stepped out of the bathroom, cleaned up, and wearing fresh clothes. "I'm assuming Craig let you out of the chains long enough to change?"

"Don't worry. Your witch's magic is strong," he assured me with a growl and held up the chain, tugging on it for emphasis. "I'm still your prisoner."

"I'd take the chain off if I knew you weren't going to try and drag my ass to your dad."

"I admit I was a bit rash at saying so, but you have to understand the position I'm in, Kate. I'm a prince of my people and you, by the laws of our land, are a traitor."

Grabbing the chain between his wrists, I dragged him along behind me towards the stairs. "And you expect me to be okay with that? I didn't even know what I was until a few days ago and you're going to be judge and jury? And what about this plague? You seem to keep forgetting what's coming to kill everyone."

"I have not forgotten, nor can I forget my duty."

"Screw your duty," I muttered, secretly hoping he'd trip as we went down the stairs.

"My duty is the same as yours."

I froze, the dragon in me lifting its head to snort in anger at him. "Don't," I warned.

"I'm merely pointing out that since you are a Darrah, your first concern should be to your clan, to the dragons," he insisted. "You might have grown up here with the humans, but you were meant to be with your own kind. Not running around with a witch and a bastard half-demon."

I tugged the chain harder, and with a curse, he stumbled over his feet down the last few stairs. "Mama Lucy saved my life. She's the one that kept me safe all these years from my own kind."

"We don't know for certain what happened that night with your father. It could have been an accident."

"An accident?" I laughed sharply. "How could it have been an accident?" I wanted to jerk on that chain so hard it made him land on his ass, or worse, hit his head on something hard.

His blank stare told me he had no idea either, and was grasping at straws. "Whether you believe me or not, I am sorry for the loss of your parents. I truly am. I do not wish to see a dragon harmed, and if you continue to let Craig guide you, you will find yourself neck deep in trouble."

"Why don't you like him?" I asked, walking to the dining table so I could pack the herbs in my knapsack. "What did he ever do to you?"

"He's a half-demon. That's enough," he scoffed, rolling his shoulders as if he could catch something from being in the same house as Craig. "And I do not approve of you being so close to him. It's not natural."

My face grew hot remembering just how close we'd been in my room, and I lowered my head.

"Why do you look guilty all of a sudden?" he asked curiously.

"I don't."

"Yes, you do." He sniffed the air around me, and I backed away, but it was too late. His sharp, narrowed gaze told me he knew Craig and I had done more than talk a few moments ago and his lip lifted in a snarl. "He has touched you."

"It's no business of yours," I snapped. "Stay out of it."

I tried to storm past him, but he caught my arm.

The same familiar jolt of belonging shot through me as it had the day on the street when I barreled into him.

My heart pounded, and my dragon sat at attention as a strange longing filled my being.

Forrest was a dragon, and now that mine was awakened, it sensed his. I felt it stirring inside his body the longer he held onto my arm. His energy thrummed against mine, and in that moment, I wasn't staring into his eyes—I stared into the eyes of his dragon.

"I know I have not made things easy," he whispered, "but I do know we must stop this plague from harming our people. I will fight for you, Kate Darrah, I will. I need you to know that."

"I want to believe you," I replied softly, my brow furrowed, "but, how can I?"

"What do you see in my eyes? Do you see an enemy?"

His bright blue eyes glimmered with the life of his dragon, and I couldn't deny the kinship he gave me. The connection I sensed between myself and Craig was different than what I felt now with Forrest. This was familiar, and on same strange level made me feel like I was home.

I blinked, and my gaze lingered over his chiseled face, how those blue eyes stood out against his darker skin.

Tattoos snaked up towards his neck and disappeared beneath the collar of his t-shirt before reappearing out of the sleeves. Markings of his clan. I knew it without having to ask. They jogged a memory in my mind, and the marks on my arms started to make sense.

All dragons were marked for the clan they belonged to, designating their bloodline. Guess mine had been made invisible by the bracelet I wore since I was a child.

Without a word, I reached up and undid the manacles around his wrists. "Don't make me regret this," I told him, and shoved the chain in my knapsack. "Just in case."

Forrest rubbed his wrists. "I will not betray you again, Kate. You have my word as a prince."

"How about you help me find the rest of the

shield and seal the plague away for good? We can worry about all the other crap later."

The dragon in me said I could trust him, even though I was still angry with him. Red flags shot up in my mind, but we needed his help. Craig wasn't from the dragon realm. Forrest was, and with him, we'd be able to find our way around faster and hopefully avoid any trouble.

I felt his eyes on me as I organized my pack just for something to do.

Craig whistled as he trudged downstairs a few minutes later and paused when he saw Forrest without the manacles. "You sure you want to do that?"

"We need him, and though he decided to be an asshole once we returned home, he did help us in the Burnt World," I pointed out. "Don't worry, I still have the chains."

I told them I was going to the kitchen to find some bottles of water, but really, I needed to get away from their stare-down. Whatever bro talk they were having without words, I did not want to be a part of it.

I had enough things to worry about, like finding a shield broken into possibly hundreds of pieces, and sealing a plague spawn back in its cage.

Yup, that was more than enough for me to deal with.

4

FORREST

Craig's eyes followed Kate as she walked to the back of the house and vanished into the kitchen.

"You're lucky," he told me. "She trusts you."

"She should trust me. I am the only one in this room who is trustworthy, to begin with."

"Seriously?"

I stepped closer, so we were only a foot apart. "I'm only going to warn you once. Stay away from her. Do not think for a moment you could ever be with her. She is a dragon and a Darrah."

"Something you seem only to care about because you deem her a traitor." He squared his shoulders as his hands closed into fists at his sides. "And Kate is a grown woman. She can choose her path."

"She is a dragon and belongs with her own."

"You're going to keep trying that line aren't you until she gives in?" He rolled his eyes and walked away. "You know if she finds out you're trying to keep me from her, she'll be pissed at you all over again."

I glanced over my shoulder towards the kitchen. "I want what's best for her."

Craig laughed. "You're serious? That's what this is about. You're jealous."

I kept a careful blank face. "No, I'm not."

"Yes, you are. You're jealous that I met her first, and that I had a moment with her first," he said, and gave a crooked smile telling me exactly what that moment entailed.

They'd kissed.

He didn't have to say it out loud. I saw the way Kate's cheeks burned when I mentioned his name. My dragon stirred within me, thinking of this foul beast touching her, but I kept myself in check.

Whatever was between them would not last long. Craig was not a warrior, not a true hero at heart. When the time came for him to fight, he would run. I knew his kind well enough. He was not in this for the long game, no matter what lies he spewed.

We would be heading to cursed lands, and there was more than just ruins there. I'd heard the haunted howling plenty of times coming from the north. The horrid sounds would drag on through the night and well onto morning. Sounds of dying dragons, their souls forever trapped by the madness that consumed their minds while they lived.

Craig continued to watch me, but I refused to rise

to the bait. If he wanted to start a fight with me, he'd have to try harder than by telling me I was jealous. Kate was a dragon, and therefore one of my clansmen. Nothing more.

Not that there could be anything more. At the end of the day, the blood of a Darrah ran in her veins whether, I wanted it to or not.

The front door opened, breaking the tension building in the room, and the witch stomped inside with Harry, two paper sacks hanging from her hands, and panic on her face.

She passed us by, set the bags on the table, and hurried off to find Kate. A few seconds later, both women returned, and the witch hastily began unpacking the bags.

"You have no more time to wait I'm afraid," the witch told us, pausing when she noticed my freed hands. "Who removed your chains?"

"I did." Lucy shot her a warning look, but Kate shrugged it off. "He might be more willing to help us if we're not having to drag his ass around. Besides, he knows what I can do now, so he'll think twice about betraying us."

How could I forget what power resided in this woman? She was fierce in human form with that sword, but as a dragon... I'd never seen dragon fire like that before. Seen the destruction it could cause. No, I would be a fool to cross Kate, at least not without a solid plan in play first.

"I hope you know what you're doing," Lucy said.

"His friends are still here so if you're going to do this, you need to do it now."

"What?" I asked.

"Four of them, saw them in town. Think I managed to dodge them, but I'm sure it won't be long before they come snooping around again." She laid out the items from the second bag, and without a word, Harry took up his watchful position at the front windows.

My nose twitched, and I breathed in the delicious scent of gold. Sitting in the center of the table was a dagger, the sheath gold, as well as the hilt, intricately carved with sapphires embedded within it. It was a magnificent piece of work, and the dragons shaped into it were in perfect detail. My hand reached out without my realizing it, but the witch snatched it up before I could.

"This is not for you," she told me sternly, and handed it to Kate.

But Kate didn't take it. "What if I get another weird vision?" she asked worriedly.

"This dagger belonged to your family. That's why it reacted the way it did." The witch offered it again, and Kate hesitated, but took it this time.

She held her breath, but after a few seconds, her brow rose, and she let out a sigh of relief.

The witch smiled. "If it called to you before, there's a chance it will again. It may come in handy."

"Great, now I have to worry about a dagger and a sword."

The witch held up a long piece of leather I realized was a sheath with a strap for a person to wear diagonally across their body that had another place on the front for a dagger. "Which is why I also brought you this."

Kate took the piece, weighing it in her hands. "I can't believe I'm doing this. It's like I'm preparing for war."

"We probably are," Craig said quietly, and Kate gulped. "Just being honest."

"Maybe be less honest." She slipped the strap over her body, and Craig went to grab the sword as I watched her attach the dagger to the sheath on the front.

She was certainly becoming more and more like a warrior than the woman that ran into me that day on the street.

Craig returned to her with the Executioner and helped sheath it at her back. His hands lingered on her shoulders a bit too long for my taste, but then he walked away, and I swallowed my jealousy down.

Craig turned to the witch. "What else did you bring?"

"Salves for healing wounds, though I pray to the goddess you won't need them. These vials here are potions to aid in fighting. Blue is for fog, red is for explosions, and the yellow is to stun. For the love of the goddess, do not mix them up," she said, and eyed us all sternly as if we were children.

"Dragons do not use potions."

Kate ground her teeth, but it was Lucy who said, "Do you really want to draw attention to yourselves by flying around and letting them all know you're there? Besides, Kate might have shifted once, but she is still new to this ability. It may not come so easily again."

"It won't?" Kate asked confused. "Why not?"

"Your dragon has been sleeping for years," she explained. "And it sounds like the last time, you were in a time of high stress. I'm assuming dragon form can be affected by mood?"

She directed the question at me, and after a second, I nodded in confirmation.

She continued, "So, you need these potions in case she can't shift. Got it?"

The three of us nodded.

"I want you all to wear these." She picked up three silver bangles I hadn't noticed yet.

When she held one out to me, I didn't take it.

"It's not going to bite you."

"What is it for?"

"To help you know where each other is. If you get separated, the bracelets will lead you back to one another."

I didn't like the idea of wearing a magical enchantment, but Craig already slipped his on, and Kate watched me closely.

Finally, I did the same. "Happy?"

"No," Lucy said, but she accepted it. "Now, I wanted to ensure you could find your way home this time, so this will create a portal, but be careful. This is powerful magic and if used incorrectly can have consequences."

The rounded object was the size of her palm and appeared to be an ancient coin. Not gold, but silver and bronze. Words were etched around it, and the image in the center was of a moon cracked down the center.

"I've heard of these," Craig said in awe. "I spent months looking for one for a buyer."

I frowned. "What is it?"

Craig tentatively reached out, and Lucy laid it in his hand.

"It's a moon door portal," he whispered, turning it over gently. "Witches use them to create portals."

"And this one is very old," Lucy said. "Do your best not to lose it, or damage it."

Craig nodded, and handed it over to Kate so she could look it over. Lucy packed the salves and other items into the knapsack, closed it, and handed it to Craig who diligently swung it onto his back. "I believe we're ready to go."

"And you should before his friends return."

Lucy eyed me disapprovingly again, but I ignored it. My men were doing as they were instructed and since their job was to guard me and I was nowhere to be found, they were searching for me. My father would know by now I had disappeared, which meant more of our men would be roaming the dragon realm than normal. Getting to the ruins would not be an easy trek.

Kate moved to the foyer, Craig standing beside her, and I took a place to the other side. Lucy hugged Kate close, and they clung to each other. I saw the worry in Lucy's eyes as she held Kate like she was her daughter. She had raised her well enough I supposed, but part of me could not forgive the witch for allowing that bracelet to remain on Kate's wrist, trapping her true form. They finally parted, and both women wiped their eyes hastily. The three of us stood in a tight circle as Kate held the portal in her hand.

"As you hold the coin, you have to think of where you want to go," Lucy instructed.

"But I've never been there," Kate said. "What if I mess it up?"

"I could get us there," I offered, trying to sound helpful and not too eager to return to my homeland.

Craig gave me a doubtful look, but I did really want us to return to the dragon world.

I glared at him. "Look, this plague is going to spread if we don't stop it. We need answers, and if those answers are at the Darrah ruins, then that's where I'll take us. I swear it."

Craig looked ready to argue, but Kate handed me the coin. "You take us anywhere else, or straight to your dad, and I'll kick your ass," she warned.

Wearing the Executioner blade on her back and

the dagger at her front, she looked like she probably could without a problem.

"I swear I will take you to the ruins." I rubbed my thumbs over the coin, feeling the power waiting to be used. "How do I make it work?"

"Focus on where you want to go," Lucy said. "Picture yourself there, picture the place."

I did that, but nothing happened. "It's not working."

She rolled her eyes. "Clearly your mind is conflicted."

"It is not," I argued.

"Then it should work. Are you sure you want to go where you said?" she challenged.

I shut my eyes, tuning out her nagging doubts and thought of where I wanted to go.

My instincts told me to go back to my home, back to the castle I left behind, but part of me rebelled. My dragon to be precise. He reared his head and growled indignantly that I could not forget all that occurred in the Burnt World. Craig and Kate saved my life when they did not have to. And Kate, she risked herself to save both of us so we could get back home. She fought a plagued demon, could've easily died, and I was considering going back on my word.

I wanted to say my father would understand our plight and aid us in this quest, but the dragon huffed in annoyance.

My father would look to his own first. He would see Craig as a means to an end and Kate as a Darrah.

As much as I told myself it had to be an accident, her father dying, the dragon in me sensed the deception. Whatever happened to her parents came back to my father's actions.

No, I had to help them and stop this plague from leaving the Burnt World and coming to the dragon one next, unless it was already there.

"Think it's working."

At Kate's words, I opened my eyes to see the coin glowing and humming with power. The words turned bright blue, and Lucy told us to hold onto one another.

She only had eyes for Kate, and I saw the silent exchange between them.

The fear Kate might not come back.

The glow from the coin grew, and Craig and Kate laid a hand on my shoulders. Soon it surrounded us, and I felt my feet leave the floor as we were removed from the witch's home and flung through the portal. Swirling blue and purple lights surrounded us, and though I couldn't see Kate or Craig, their hands dug into my shoulders. We twisted and turned until I thought I was going to be sick.

When the lights faded, we collapsed in a heap, hitting solid ground with a thud. I grimaced as my head hit harder than the rest of me and I opened my eyes.

"Are we in the right place?" Kate asked, sitting beside me and looking around curiously.

I sat up, holding my throbbing head, and nodded.

"Welcome to Gregornath," I said, "home of the dragon clans."

"And where exactly are we?" Craig asked.

I glanced around and tried to get my bearings, my head still throbbing making it hard to focus. "We should be on the outskirts of the capital. A few miles at least, away from anyone who might see us. Why?"

"Because someone's already seen us," he growled. "And they're coming this way."

5

KATE

"What?" I whipped my head around towards the direction Craig was looking. "That doesn't sound promising."

The thundering of horse hooves pounded our direction, and Craig hauled me to my feet. He did the same for Forrest, but the second Forrest stood, punched him hard in the face, sending him flying backward.

"What the bloody hell type of game are you playing at?" Craig growled and brought his fist back for another hit.

I caught his arm and shoved them apart from each other. "Can we get out of sight before you two try to kill each other?"

"He's already betrayed us!"

"It's a patrol," Forrest explained quickly, rubbing his jaw and glowering at Craig. "They probably felt a disturbance in the air and are coming to investigate as they should, since they've also probably received word that their prince has gone missing."

The horses were getting closer, and as the guys bickered like children, I searched for a place to hide.

There was a rock outcropping not too far from the place we landed and with them still snapping at each other's throats, I grabbed them both by an ear and tugged them out of sight. They winced and tried to pull away, but I only held on tighter, then tossed them to the ground behind the rocks.

My newfound strength was coming in handy already.

"Shut it, both of you," I warned, when Forrest opened his mouth again.

His eyes narrowed, but he fell silent.

I peeked my head over the rocks, careful to use the bit of brush around us to hide, and watched as five horses came to a stop where'd we landed. They studied something on the ground, and I worried they would find a way to track us.

One by one, they hopped off their horses and looked our direction. I ducked down quickly, cursing.

"We have to move," I whispered.

Forrest studied our surroundings and nodded. "Follow me, stay close."

He took off, staying bent over, and I quickly followed with Craig right behind me. We wove our way through the trees, but I could hear the dragon soldiers behind us.

My pulse pounded in my ears drowning everything else out as my dragon lifted her head, ready to strike. I felt the change start to come over me, and suddenly Forrest reached back, took a firm hold of my hand, and my dragon settled down.

I let him keep hold of me as he led us on, down a short slope to a creek.

We stomped through it and then veered sharply to the left up another rocky slope to where a dark grove of trees grew. We huddled close and waited, listening intently for any sign of them following.

Forrest's hand was warm on mine, and I felt his race pulsing as strongly as mine was.

The soldiers grew closer, I shut my eyes, willing them to look the other way, to not find us, but the sound of water splashing made me open my eyes.

"The trail ends here," a rough voice yelled. "Spread out and send word back to Kadin! We may have intruders!"

"We can't just sit here," Craig whispered. "They'll find us."

Forrest let go of my hand, and my dragon mourned the loss of his strong touch before I scolded myself for thinking of anything, but escaping these dragons.

He was brushing at something on the ground, and I frowned, wondering what he was up to, when I saw the edges of a wooden door.

Carefully, he opened it a crack and motioned for us to jump down. Craig flat out refused to do it, but we were running out of time. Before he could stop me, I swung my legs over the dark pit and dropped down.

It was a bit further than I anticipated and swallowed a surprised yelp when I hit the ground hard.

Forrest dropped down after me and moved back to the opening to hold up Craig's legs long enough so he could quietly close the trap door.

Then he dropped him, and Craig flailed his arms, trying not to land on his head.

"Are you done now?" I demanded, surprised I could see their outlines in the darkness. "How can I see?"

"We're able to see in the dark," Forrest replied. "Partially, at least."

I heard fumbling, and saw Craig digging around in the knapsack. A bright beam of light came on a second later, and he waved the flashlight around us.

The tunnel was made of stone and mud, filled with cobwebs and the spiders to go along with them. I shuddered and instinctively moved closer to them and away from the dangling webs.

"Where are we?" Craig asked, shining the light in one direction then another, where it was swallowed up by the darkness.

"Old tunnels. They run underneath most of the clans' territories."

"Why? I didn't think dragons would like to be underground?" I asked.

Forrest grunted in agreement, and I saw the beads

of sweat on his forehead. "We don't, at least most of us don't."

I guessed growing up in the human world made me less prone to being uncomfortable when away from the open sky. I didn't like it, but I could stand it if it would keep us out of sight. "How close will these take us to the Darrah lands?" I asked.

"Within a few leagues, but that's open territory. It's going to be difficult to sneak around once we reach the end of the line," he explained.

"Dragons still patrol the area?" I frowned. "Why?"

"Because stupid children like me and my friend will try to go to them. And to keep any others from stumbling into them unknowingly."

"Or to keep the truth hidden from your people," Craig mumbled.

Forrest growled, and though I couldn't see the smoke coming out of his nose, I smelled it, sharp and acrid. "My father does not lie to our people."

"No? So, Maddock Darrah was not one of your people?"

"Guys, just stop," I growled, and moved between them.

Craig immediately lowered the beam of light he'd been shining purposely right into Forrest's eyes.

I exhaled. "We'll deal with that later, but right now we need to keep moving. I have a feeling we're going to be walking quite a way."

Forrest nodded in agreement, and rolled his tense

shoulders. "Indeed. It'd be a shame to lose someone along the way."

"If you touch each other," I interrupted, as Craig growled, "I'll duct tape your hands and your mouths, and yes, I brought it with me. A girl never knows what she's going to need, so watch it, both of you."

Forrest glowered at me, but bowed his head.

Craig smirked as he said, "I like this slightly crazy Kate. Suits you very well."

I rolled my eyes, but grinned with him. "You've got the light, so get going."

He stepped around us and led the way down the tunnel.

I wanted to run so we could get out of here faster, but the ground was extremely uneven with rocks, and where the dirt had come through the stones that held it back, keeping it from crushing us. I imagined it, the tunnels shaking and the old stones giving way, swallowing us up in the darkness. We'd be buried alive, and no one would ever find us.

I gulped and shivered at the thought when a warm hand slipped into mine.

"You have to control your dragon, especially down here," Forrest whispered.

"I'm trying, but all I keep seeing is us being buried."

"These stones have held for centuries. The tunnels are safe," he promised, squeezing my hand.

Though I felt my dragon shift and move, she settled down, watchful, but not as agitated as before.

"How do you do that?" I whispered. "Get it to calm down?"

"Years of training and practice."

"Great. I don't have that," I muttered, and longed for the time back with my dad, or at least all the lessons he taught me. No matter how hard I tried to remember, it was just a blur of faces and voices, nothing to show me exactly what I wanted. "I'm going to get us all killed."

"No, you won't. I won't let you do anything you'll regret later."

His words came out in a growl as he spoke them, and I noticed him glaring at the back of Craig's skull.

I gave his hand a hard tug and arched my brow at him. "Stop."

"I can't help it. Instinct."

Craig was far ahead of us, but I was pretty sure he could hear without a problem. Talking about him probably wouldn't bother him with the way he was, but it bothered me.

I was conflicted between Craig and Forrest, trusting them both and drawn to them both. It was horrible and incredible at the same time.

I hated it.

"What happened between the demons and dragons anyway?" I asked, hoping the conversation would distract me from the dangling spider webs catching in my hair, and another portion of stones that protruded from the wall, dirt falling around them.

The stones shifted right beside me near the floor, and I flinched away, grabbing hold of Forrest.

"Our feud is old," he started talking, thankfully, and I focused on the growling sound of his voice that seemed so familiar and comforting. "And the dragons aren't the only ones who have issues with the demons."

"Why? Are they that bad? Craig's not."

"Craig is half-demon and though I will admit I have a hard time… really seeing it," he said slowly, "he would make a good ruler of his people, if they would let him live."

"They hate him?"

"He is half-demon, therefore weak in their eyes. Not worth living. Many of us knew of the only son the demon king had, a bastard half-demon," he whispered. "We also heard of the pain inflicted upon him by his own family."

I blinked and saw the scars on Craig's back before my eyes. I wondered how many other scars covered the rest of his body and understood his sharp humor and quick tongue were his defense mechanism against a world that wouldn't accept him.

I chewed on my lip. "Even if he finds a way to stop this plague from spreading, you don't think they'll change their minds?"

"His people don't know about the plague, or at least not all of them. According to what Craig's said, Raghnall is hiding the truth, making excuses."

"Why would he do that if he knows it's killing his people?"

Forrest offered up a shrug. "Why indeed?"

"But the fighting, did someone kill someone from the other side?"

I waited a long few minutes for him to answer.

His hand grew warmer in mine, and he finally nodded. "There were several assassinations carried out, killing many of the dragons on the council for all the races. We suspected demons, but nothing could be proven. One of them was my mother and my oldest sister, along with her husband."

I leaned into him for comfort, murmuring quietly, "I'm so sorry."

"It was a long time ago, but thank you."

"But you can't blame Craig for what happened," I added. "He spent his whole life fighting to survive, I doubt they sent him to kill your family."

He grunted. "I know they did not, but old hatreds run deep. There were more deaths amongst the other races long before my family, and yet nothing could be proven." He kicked angrily at a rock near his feet. "Raghnall became the head of the council after the incidences, and the demons have held a majority ever since. They are the richest amongst us, claim lands for themselves when they believe no one is looking, and we received word not too long ago they are forging weapons."

"Is that a bad thing?" I asked, shaking my head

confused. "I have a feeling that's how you guys protect yourselves here."

"Enough weapons for an army no race is supposed to have standing," he amended.

"Oh. You think he's preparing for war?"

"Yes," a voice answered, but it wasn't Forrest.

Craig had stopped walking, and I hadn't even noticed.

His gaze slipped to Forrest holding my hand, and his eyes darkened, but he said nothing about it. "Raghnall has been preparing for the ultimate war for decades, which is probably why he's lying about the plague."

I felt the need to apologize, but when he turned that gaze on me, it was smiling with amusement.

God, he was so damned cocky, my holding hands with Forrest didn't even bother him.

I let go of Forrest's hand, all the same.

"Why'd we stop?" Forrest asked.

"Split, up ahead, and the right side is caved in."

I swallowed hard as my fear grew again, my dragon unsettled and moving inside. "I thought you said these tunnels would hold?" I whispered, trying not to panic.

"They should," Forrest said as he walked ahead, taking the light from Craig.

"You two have a nice chat?" Craig asked, leaning in close to whisper in my ear.

"I think we did. Does that bother you?"

He winked and gave a deep rumble of laughter.

"Whatever suits you best, love, is alright by me, but we both know he's too stuck up for you."

I wanted to argue, but a voice in my head said he was right. Deep down, I sensed part of my close connection to Forrest was merely because we were both dragons and I'd been away from my kind far too long. Head in shambles with too many thoughts and feelings to keep track of, I kept my mouth shut.

"Something closed in the tunnel," Forrest said as Craig and I approached.

"Something? Not someone?" I stared at the collapsed tunnel to the right. "How can you tell?"

"I can smell it."

I sniffed the air and coughed harshly. "What is that?" I gasped, rubbing my nose, trying to get the horrible musty stench out of it.

"Something I hoped we would avoid. If we go this way, we'll wind up above ground sooner, and it'll take a bit longer to get there, but we don't have a choice."

"How many patrols are usually out?" Craig asked.

"Enough to give us trouble if we're not careful." Forrest's lips thinned. "Let's keep moving. Once we're out of the tunnels, we'll find a safe place to rest up and trudge on."

He led the way this time, and I followed, Craig, bringing up the rear.

The air around us changed drastically. Both of them were tense, and when I glanced back, Craig had his hand on one of his daggers at his hip. I knew he had a few more tucked out of sight, but did not like that he suddenly felt the need to have it at the ready.

"What exactly are we worried about running into?" I whispered. "Guys?"

Forrest sighed and stopped. "Fractorns."

"Bless you," I mumbled, and Craig sniggered.

"You find this amusing?" Forrest snapped at Craig.

"The name, yes, but what it actually is? No. I've seen the pictures."

"Can someone tell me what the hell a fractorn is?"

Forrest aimed the beam of light down to the floor, and it took a second, but slowly the prints came into view. They appeared to be that of a bear paw, but the claws were so long, they dug into the dirt a few inches, and the paw was twice the size of a bear's. Another claw imprint came out the back of the paw, and when Forrest lifted the beam of light overhead, I saw that every few feet, there was a hole in the stones along with deep groove marks as if something sharp dragged across and penetrated the stone as it moved.

I gulped, and reached for the dagger at my chest. "What does it like to eat?"

"Anything that moves." Forrest shone the light around the tunnel and everywhere I looked, I saw signs of a large, furry beast having passed this way. "They usually hibernate this time of year, and I've never heard of them being in the tunnels."

I flinched. "Awesome."

Craig gave me a gentle nudge onwards when Forrest started walking again.

"Best to keep moving and get out of here," Craig whispered.

It was all the encouragement I needed to move quicker. We covered a good amount of ground, until Forrest said up ahead there would be a large opening and beyond that, another tunnel that would lead us out into the fresh air.

Suddenly, Forrest shut off the light and cursed, throwing out his hand to stop me.

"What?" I hissed.

He shook his head fiercely, putting a finger to his lips, pointed into the cavern.

My gut dropped to the floor. Mentally, I was flinging every curse in the book. Outwardly, I was grabbing the dagger so hard, my knuckles turned white.

There, filling the cavern, were a sleeping group of these fractorns.

Across the open space, I could see the other tunnel, but there was no way we were getting passed without waking them up.

We were trapped.

I hope you enjoyed *Rivals*!
Look for Book Two: *Shards*

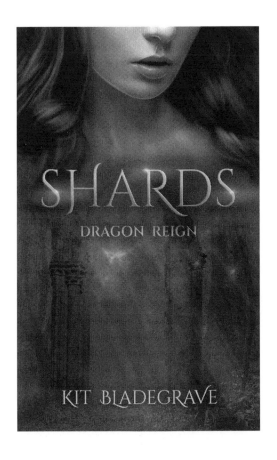

For Kit's Newsletter put the following in a browser window:

mailerlite.com/webforms/landing/m5q3f7